THE CAGE

OTHER CLARION BOOKS
BY ROY BROWN

Find Debbie!

The White Sparrow

No Through Road

Escape the River

a novel by **ROY BROWN**

THE CAGE

A Clarion Book | **The Seabury Press** | New York

The Seabury Press, 815 Second Avenue, New York, N.Y. 10017

First American edition 1977
Copyright © 1976 by Roy Brown
This book was first published in Great Britain in 1976
by Abelard-Schuman London Limited
Printed in the United States of America

Library of Congress Cataloging in Publication Data

Brown, Roy.
The cage.

"A Clarion book."
SUMMARY: A group of teenage boys plan an escape when they realize their
imprisonment is part of an experiment to repattern their personalities.
[1. Behavior modification—Fiction. 2. Psychological fiction] I. Title.
PZ7.B81693Cag3   [Fic]   77-1586
ISBN 0-8164-3198-1

THE CAGE

1

HE AWOKE.

He was strapped to the ceiling of a small, strange room; arms, legs, and neck pinioned—painlessly but with a total restriction.

He could see down into the well of the room, at the bottom of which was a curiously bowl-shaped floor absorbing faint light through a grille: not the harsh spill of a lamp but the stealthy intrusion of dawn—or twilight?

His own dawn—that of returning consciousness—switched on like a charge of current. Suddenly the bizarre topsy-turviness of his position reversed itself and he knew that he was lying on a bed gazing not *down* but *up*. It was the ceiling which was curved, like the bone-colored and slightly wrinkled concave interior of a giant skull. The fragment of daylight leaked through a high, narrow window lacing the ceiling with bar-shadows.

A *prison* cell?

A second question arrived—more urgent, more electric with its shock of alarm: not *where am I?* but *who am I?*

Steady . . . steady, he thought. The answer would come. Give it time! He was still not fully awake, that was all.

He didn't try to sit up at once but carried out a few cautious tests on himself, like an accident victim who fears his back may be broken. Fingers then toes. There was no pain, nor tell-tale numbness—they wriggled freely inside what was evidently a sleeping bag. The fingers touched and probed, discovering nothing amiss with the rest of his body—thighs, stomach, chest . . .

A few seconds of this were enough. He soon grew bolder and eased himself up on his elbows. Yes, a sleeping bag of greenish quilting, not new. His head had rested on a pillow slipped inside a gray cover filled—or so he guessed—with bits of rubber or plastic foam. The bed was narrow and firm-springed. There was a mattress, hard and covered with the same coarse fabric as the pillow.

He lay back again and let his eyes make an inventory: floor of uneven flagstones with a plain, rectangular straw mat beside the bed on his right. The cell measured about eight feet square, eight high. Its totally bare walls were of rough stone, giving off a faint smell like cheap whitewash. In one corner stood a small, plain locker and a four-legged stool.

There was an arched door, heavily constructed of iron-bound panels. It was latched, with a large keyhole beneath. He unzipped the sleeping bag, pulled himself free of it and sat on the bed with his bare feet on the straw mat. He was dressed only in a gray tee shirt and pants. He could see no other clothes, no shoes or socks.

He sat there for some moments in his private and mysterious limbo. Still the furniture of his mind was as sparse as that of the cell. No more awakening, no more discoveries, *nothing*. Nothing but the ordinary mechanism of sense and touch: hard was hard; soft was soft; light was light; skin shivered . . . but he *remembered* nothing. Who had built that wall in his brain?

And *who was he?*

He looked for a long time at his hands as if they might yield an answer. He brought them up to his face, an unremembered face with a stranger's down of beard. Yet the touch brought a tantalizing promise of self-discovery as if he were in a boat drifting toward a fog-bound beach. Perhaps . . . if he could see into a mirror . . .

But the cell had no looking glass. He crossed dizzily to the locker and flung open the cupboard: socks, a gray denim suit, handkerchiefs, a pair of canvas shoes, two gray shirts. In the drawer above was a toothbrush, a tablet of plain soap and a small flashlight of white metal, battery in good order.

No labels on anything, no name tags.

And no sanitation, not even a chamber pot! He'd have to call a guard soon. . . . When would they bring his breakfast?

Or would it be supper?

Who were *they?* Who was *he?* What had he *done?*

His brain tried to grapple with the questions, racing like a pulse beat as he pulled on his drab shirt and uniform suit. Not a bad fit. Shoes too. During that deep sleep somebody—*they?*—must have measured him as if for a coffin.

Hell, it was getting dark. It was not morning after all but evening—and there was no light switch, only the little flashlight.

After a bit, maddened by the silence, he crossed to the door and shouted. He rattled the latch. He banged the heavy panels repeatedly with his fists, then kicked them until the balls of his feet stung.

No response. No footfall outside. No jangling of keys.

Eventually he gave up, sat on the edge of his bed. When he put his chin in his hands, the down was damp with sweat.

Steady . . . *steady* . . . they'll come. They must. Otherwise he'd have to urinate in the corner! Yet something in his unknown identity recoiled with an instinctive fastidiousness. He could wait.

What should he do next? He gave the simple question long and tedious thought. His brief violence on the door had exhausted him, temporarily stemming the flood of horror. He probed on into his dark half-brain, trying to remember; trying to forge some connection between past and present, act and consequence. But there was no data and, suddenly, no real concern, only a listless curiosity.

His eyes languidly measured the height of the darkening window, then he glanced at the stool. His arms were almost too weak to embrace it, pick it up, and carry it across the cell.

His mood changed once more. He felt a sudden surge of petulance and flung the stool away. It struck the door and disintegrated, legs and struts rattling away like drumsticks.

That would bring them running! A long minute passed— a minute of total silence, and still nobody came.

With greater deliberation he dragged the locker beneath the window instead and laboriously climbed on to it. Now his face was level with the deep, stone inset. The barred frame held a single sheet of frosted glass and was open on its pivots, just an inch or so, presumably for ventilation. It was quite impossible to open it farther and through the narrow gap at the bottom he could glimpse only a thin strip of anonymous stonework.

He saw no point in trying to smash the glass. Instead he hung there, head twisted awkwardly, listening for sounds. Not far off a bird sang; a thrush? How did he guess it was a thrush? Then, closer still, the skuttle of some small creature above his head. A bat?

He felt soft wind on his face—a wind that brought no secret from the coming night. He groped his way down, meticulously replaced the locker, then slumped back on his bed.

He uttered the two words to himself aloud, over and over again: "Thrush, bat; thrush, bat . . ." As if encouraged, his brain began to chatter as automatically as a teleprinter. He let more words come to his lips as faithfully as a well-programmed robot:

"Shall I compare thee to a summer's day?

Thou art more lovely and more temperate . . ."

"Oh to be in England now that April's there . . ."

"*Question:* What is your name?

Answer: ??????

Question: Who gave you this name?

Answer: My godfathers and godmothers in my baptism wherein I was made a member of Christ, a child of God and an inheritor of the Kingdom of Heaven.

Question: What did your godfathers and godmothers then do for you?

Answer: They did promise and vow three things in my name . . .

What name, for chrissake? Why do I remember all this stuff—Shakespeare, Browning, the Catechism, and not my own bloody name?

Without warning a new spasm of senseless fury seized him by the throat—fury and fright—and he flung himself screaming at the door of the cell, yanked at the latch until his fingers bled, shouted blasphemies—and suddenly the door opened!

Only then, in a moment of sanity, did he realize that he had never actually tried to open it. He had *assumed* the door would be locked.

Beyond, the darkness was intensified so he went back for the flashlight. He found himself in a corridor and stood and listened for a few moments—realized he was listening only to the panting of his own breath. He fed the beam of the light to the darkness.

The unlit stone passage continued for an unknown distance in each direction. At once the beam picked up a row of doors on the same side as his own. Across the passage the wall was broken here and there by arches giving access down flights of stone steps to dim and dusty depths. The foundations of the building? *What* building?

He shrank from the adventure of exploring and turned his attention instead to the other doors. He counted four identical to his own, each closed, each with the same arched design: *Gothic?* He murmured the word to himself, hoping it would prove a key to unlock a new fragment of memory; but, like his other verbal dredgings, it stood obdurately on its own, pointing nowhere.

What of these names, though?

Each door bore a piece of reassuringly ordinary white card, apparently glued to the panels. His beam picked them out one by one, and the names shaped themselves on his lips:

HACKETT WHEELER O'MALLEY RAXBY SKEEL.

Idiot! He had closed his own cell door behind him.
Which was *his?*
He started at the beginning of the row. At each door he knocked, listened, paused, lifted the latch and pushed. The cells were practically identical—bed, locker, barred window, straw mat—and bore no sign of occupation. The third

door, the one in the middle, bumped against the bits of broken stool. O'Malley's cell!

So his name was *O'Malley?*

He shone the flashlight on the card for a long time—as if the precious name was in gilt letters.

He—O'Malley—checked the other two cells, found them deserted. Then, as if even this tenuous hint of identity had emboldened him, he tried out a set of those stone steps into the depths. Who would care if he relieved his bladder there?

And he was lost at once—lost and confused. The steps melted away into a series of close-packed arches, each one a dark mirror image of the next. Whichever way the beam flickered, it met only an opaqueness of stone.

Soon he found himself dropping to his knees, crawling, coughing, groping for a space that utterly eluded him. Then, just as the new terror of claustrophobia clawed at him, there was a sound—one which registered an ironic familiarity.

It was the flush of a toilet.

Somebody had pulled a chain. Somebody *else* was here.

O'MALLEY CRAWLED OFF TOWARD THE SOUND, ABRUPTLY
and impetuously, and struck his forehead on a granite-hard
edge. He swore, feeling blood trickle down his face.

Half-blinded, he found the washroom at the top of some
steps. At first he was merely aware of having arrived at an
archway with a room-space beyond. He crouched before
entering and switched off the flashlight. He listened.

There was the drip, drip, drip of faulty plumbing; and
when he saw the electric light, he ducked lower, gripping
his flashlight like a club, expecting some assault, some
challenge.

Still nothing, no one.

He moved on in, the smell of strong disinfectant in his
nostrils. The light came from a single dusty, unshaded electric bulb hanging from the ceiling, but he could find no
switch. Beneath a high slit of barred window was a short
row of open urinals, and he realized that the cistern he had
heard supplied the troughs, automatically flooding them at
intervals when the supply tank above was replenished.

Hell, was his prison as fully automated as it was deserted? What next, O'Malley—a tray of eggs and bacon on
a conveyor belt?

He suddenly felt drained of concern, only responsive to

creature needs. He used one of the urinals. At once the cistern obligingly flooded it, squirting brownish water, reeking of carbolic acid, into the cracked porcelain. Behind him were two cubicles fitted with half-doors swung open to expose the toilet seats—small, fitted at a low level. Not a very cozy place!

He helped himself to pink paper from a roll, experimentally pulled the chain, and watched more of the brown water flush into the bowl.

Next to the closets was a shower cubicle hung across with a slightly torn plastic curtain. A brief twist of a serrated knob wet his sleeve with what smelled like almost pure disinfectant. Likewise the water from three cold taps in the wash basins beside the urinals.

A printed card announced:

NOT FIT FOR DRINKING.

You joking?

Each basin had a holder packed with white tissue. His head was still bleeding, so he made a paper wad, wetted it and pressed it against the wound. How bad was it? He thought he could feel swelling—and the carbolic stung.

As soon as he moved away, he encountered the stranger.

The wall beside the wash basins provided a further facility: a looking glass—very old, with the silver backing badly flaked away in places, so that the mirror offered a dim, distorted image.

This was O'Malley? Blue, dulled eyes; nose slightly long, mouth rather small, stubble of fairish beard; long, straw-colored hair, pale cheeks streaked with blood . . .

He composed himself and said, "Hi, O'Malley, if that's who you are!"

The bleeding had stopped. He mopped at the unfamiliar face with more of the tissue. He fed this to one of the little toilets, then looked round for a drinking fountain.

No dice! A new apprehension, a foolhardy and brief disregard of the warning notice, a scorched tongue, a disgusted spit into the basin. . . .

No, they *weren't* joking.

Bitter-mouthed, bravado wearing thin, he didn't notice a different, more sensible route away from the washroom but groped back down the steps.

This time, instead of his head, it was the flashlight that cracked itself against a wall and fell to pieces, plunging him into total darkness. He scrabbled around to retrieve the parts; battery, bulb holder, lens. He found them, but his shaking hands couldn't manage the reassembly job.

He was now buried alive with an imagined spatter of stones on his coffin lid. His mind became a confused whirl of waking nightmares and fancies: he was an embryo in search of a womb, a parasite without a host, a disembodied brain. For uncountable minutes reason and insanity fought for scraps of truth like two dogs.

It was by chance that he stumbled at last upon more steps. He crawled up, sat cross-legged against a wall and got the pieces of the flashlight together. The switch responded, cleaving the darkness, exposing the row of cell doors.

O'Malley's should have been in the middle. He'd already pushed at the latch when the beam swept at the label—and delivered a new enigma: LANDERS.

Landers? The wrong passage, then! Yes, *all* the names were different along here:

MILLER CONWAY LANDERS BAINBRIDGE TRAVERS

O'Malley opened each door and gave the austere vacancies a swish of his beam.

That strange ebb and flow of mood: terror, irony, curiosity, indifference . . .

A sudden calm logic now. Simple . . . he'd crawled clean through the foundations of this place and accidentally hit upon a *second* passage on the other side. Very clever, O'Malley!

Where to now? Back to the washroom? At least there was some sort of steady light there: he'd sit on one of those little toilet seats and think it all out again. Anyway, what did it matter whether he found his own cell or not? *They* had given him a wide choice of beds—and why not attach a different name to this zombie who was *him*?

For chrissake, what about food—and drink? Mostly drink. The bastards!

He made his wobbly legs take him along the passage, flashlight already beginning to dim, beam scouring a golden pathway on gray stone.

It was a minute or two before he thought: Well done, O'Malley—you're getting yourself lost again.

He found himself at the foot of a stone well, not more than three feet square. On approaching it, he'd had the impression that it led to some sort of opening and switched off his light. The area, at the far end of this second passage, retained a hint of light: a greenish phosphorescence shed from the distant top of a shaft.

O'Malley ducked his head under a stone face, having to stoop a little, then he was gazing up at a square of luminosity—like thick bottle glass bathed in moonlight.

There was no sound, no movement, so he clicked the flashlight on again and let the rays crawl up the interior stonework.

Not a well; a chimney, perhaps? No narrowing into flues, however. A ventilator, then? Too big, too wide. No footholds, stonework clean and smooth.

And he was leaning on a metal frame, cold to the touch. He shone the light down.

At his feet stood a rough-hewn, shallow platform of stout timbers. Bolted to each corner was a metal strut, and the four tubular pieces bent and converged toward a welded hook in the center. Several containers rested on the platform.

So this was used as a delivery shaft—the green glass at the top could only be a hatch. A rope or chain would be fixed to the hook, then shaken free after its ascent—leaving behind no Jacob's ladder to be climbed.

When had this little bounty been sent down—and by whom? O'Malley tucked the flashlight under his chin so that both hands were free. A large cardboard box with no markings contained plain packages of soap, detergents, toothpaste—even wooden clothespins. A more shallow container yielded three small and odd-shaped loaves of bread, crusty but new-baked, still slightly warm.

There were paper cups, a dozen or more stacked inside each other, lying beside the loaves. Another box revealed butter or margarine and an additional package giving off the pungent smell of rancid cheese.

There were several apples bearing the more fragrant scent of an unknown orchard. No plates, knives, forks or spoons—but a bundle of thin wooden spatulas; an unlabelled pot of honey and, last of all, a small metal churn, spotlessly clean, containing a couple of pints of tepid and slightly curdled milk.

They weren't giving a party, but it was better than starving. O'Malley propped his light on the box of detergents and helped himself to a drink. The milk—goat's?—was unpleasant, but he gladly gulped down two paper cupfuls and wanted a third. Then, remembering the names on the doors, he put the cup back.

No, this couldn't all be for him. The others . . . which, when? He broke off a piece of the bread, smeared it with butter, unscrewed the pot of honey, and dug in a spatula. He wolfed it down, ignoring the cheese.

Finally, he rammed an apple into a trouser pocket, had a second thought, helped himself to one of the tubes of toothpaste and a spare bar of soap.

Then he shone the light again—to the top of the shaft and down the walls, letting the rays hover for a questioning moment over the platform.

And suddenly the wildness came back: terror, fury, an urge to mindless violence . . .

He bent his head under the stone face and yelled up the shaft. He shouted obscenities, a snatch from a ribald song. He picked up one of the little loaves and tried to hit the moonlit hatch with it. It came bounding back from silence into silence.

Afterward he felt sick and vaguely ashamed. And very drowsy.

He couldn't remember finding his cell. He was lying on top of the sleeping bag, shivering with the night's cold.

He began to worry, senselessly, about the time. Why hadn't he a watch? Had *they* taken it? What time was it? What day of the week? What month of the year? *What year?*

Oh, come on, O'Malley! You can do better than that. If you can spout bits of Browning and Shakespeare, surely you can remember the bloody date?

Calm again. Why this switch of mood? What was going on in that lost brain of his?

Very slowly and carefully, the words stumbling forth into the darkness, he began to recite the Catechism:

"*Question:* What is your name?

Answer: O'Malley!

Question: Who gave you this name?

Answer: My godfathers and godmothers in my baptism . . ."

The dark walls of the cell received this offering without comment, without echo.

He didn't know how long he slept. Was it still the same day—the same night?

When he next awoke, someone was sobbing, sobbing . . . O'Malley lay there listening detachedly, bemused. Then he felt the wet dripping down his cheek into his stubble and knew that it was *he* who was crying.

The cell was utterly dark. He looked up at his high barred window, but even the stars had gone out.

"O'Malley," he said to himself over and over. "O'Malley . . ." The name—his name?—was half a prayer of thanksgiving, a single small rock to which he clung.

He was aware of a hard lump in his pocket. The apple! He tugged it out, removed the toothpaste and soap as well, then dropped everything to the floor.

His next sleep was not so troubled.

3

HIS CELL WINDOW SPREAD A RIBBED FAN OF BRIGHTER light across the wrinkled ceiling. The tiniest movement out there would have broken the pattern with a shadow, but there was none.

Then the silence, so nearly absolute in this place, was interrupted by the far-off chatter of a machine: a tractor, a corn cutter? A memory stirred in O'Malley's waking brain, only to slip away as through soapy hands . . .

He swung his feet off the bed, put them on the straw mat, trod on the flashlight, which lay there next to the abandoned apple.

He was still fully dressed except for his shoes, but the night's chill seemed to have penetrated every stitch. He stamped his feet, jogged around the small cell.

He felt calmer this morning: no horrors, no petulance, and a fair recall of the previous day, remembered incidents and situations creating little oases of new identity surrounded by oblivion. He might have been a tadpole swimming in a stone jar.

He'd better take a look at that head: the bump felt like a smallish pumpkin, and there was a ridge of congealed blood over his right eye, more on the gray pillow—and what was for breakfast?

Something stirred beyond the cell door—the sound was like the breach bolt of a firearm. His eyes stayed fixed in fascination on the door and then, as he crept toward it, the black latch bar moved!

O'Malley jumped for it like a cat and planted his hand on the bar, simultaneously wedging a foot sideways against the bottom. He pressed his ear to the panel and listened. Nothing . . .

Why not take a look, O'Malley? Scared? Yes . . . of a phantom which didn't declare itself but, at the least resistance, evidently withdrew on soft feet—as if this place hadn't ghosts enough!

He waited for his heart to stop pounding, sitting on the edge of his bed and chewing through the apple, keeping his eyes on the latch. But it didn't move again—had it ever?

When he had got down to the core he made up his mind, collected soap and toothpaste and pulled open the door.

No ghost, no jailer; the dim passage was deserted. He couldn't, however, rid himself of a sense of not being alone any more and closed his cell door behind him with a new furtiveness.

It seemed simple this morning to find the right route to the washroom—creeping past two cell doors, along to the end of the passage, then turning, his eyes feeding on the faintly spilling daylight, ears tuned to the gurgles and drips.

He could see now that the second passage began on the other side of the washroom entrance; the steps he'd blundered up and down last night yawned on his right.

The electric bulb hung cold, but there was sunshine

| 24 |

glancing through the barred window slit. O'Malley greeted his reflection—a shade healthier today, despite the bump and blood. But the black eye peered out of the glass and the gaze seemed to be trying to tell him something.

"Say, O'Malley," he said. "They sent us on quite a trip!"

He rolled up his shirt sleeves to wash, glanced down at his arms, saw the series of tiny scabs . . . and again memory tried to turn a key in his brain. There was nothing more, though—except that when he'd doused himself with the stinking cold water and dried his hands he carefully buttoned the sleeves back.

Then he spotted the soap—a bar identical to his, lying on the ledge of a second basin streaked with grime. There was also a wad of tissue, screwed up, lying on the floor beneath.

And a sound came from behind, which O'Malley hadn't noticed till now: the dying chuckle of a tank from one of the cubicles. The half door stood open and the chain was still swinging.

He went back, much more quietly, to the cells on his own side. Feeling more angry than afraid, he was not at all stealthy. He banged at a couple of the doors in turn and thrust them open.

He struck gold with the second, the one labelled *Raxby*. The mattress was askew, the sleeping bag spilled on the floor, the drawer of the locker open.

O'Malley closed the door, stood outside for a moment, then had a sudden instinct. He opened his own cell.

The figure squatting on the bed was swarthy and thick-set; huge shoulders, big hands, startled eyes almost black and slightly hooded; mouth open, showing rough-stained teeth and forming a nervous grin.

"Hope you don't mind the liberty, mate."

"Be my guest," said O'Malley.

Another uncertain grin. "I've been wandering about. Woke up late. Found the john. Tried a few doors and got nowhere fast. Couldn't find nobody . . . I thought this door was locked, first time round."

"It sticks a bit," said O'Malley, admitting nothing.

"I should have hollered." The figure half got up. "Want your cell back?" He had a tendency to talk out of the corner of his mouth.

"No hurry."

The boy's eyes were full of unasked questions. "You don't happen to have any cigarettes?" O'Malley, leaning against the door, shook his head. "Name's Raxby. You're O'Malley, right? How long you been in?"

"In? Oh . . . since yesterday."

"Excused from duties, are you?" His eyes were sly: not quite confession time for Raxby, decided O'Malley. In his brash fashion he was trying to bluff, hoping O'Malley would tell him what he wanted to know.

But he let Raxby flounder on in search of his own little pool of reason.

"I mean, everybody else is out on a work gang, right? And the guards have gone along with them."

Raxby might have been watching an ant crawl on O'Malley's shoulder. "How come you got left behind? Trouble? Looks like there's been a real punch up here! How many of the guards did you manage to clobber with that stool— before they beat hell out of you? I know you Irish!"

O'Malley shook his head. Raxby watched him, weight creaking on the bed springs. He had a look of belligerence at first—then surrender. "I get it—you're in the same boat as me. I was only trying that work gang caper for size.

What's happened to us, mate?"

"We're . . . suffering from amnesia."

"So that's it. I woke up with a head like a turnip. Couldn't remember a thing. How I got in that cell, tucked in bed in my shorts . . . didn't know what my name was— only found that out when I spotted the label on the door. And I couldn't remember where I'd come from, even my own face. Until I found the john, and took a look in that mirror, I could have been a bleeding parrot for all I knew." He waited. "You too?"

"Yes . . ."

"So the guards never bashed you?"

"I bumped into a wall in the dark."

"What happened to the stool?"

"I . . . chucked it about."

The fellow was good-natured now, more relaxed, but he was breathing through flared nostrils. "Yeah . . . well, I know how you felt, mate. If I hadn't come across you this morning, I'd have busted everything in sight." He was still a sleep-walker in search of familiar stairs. "So what do you figure the score is?"

"A drug, I think."

"Drug!" For Raxby this was evidently a worse indignity than being struck down with a blunt instrument. "So that's it. We'd better get ourselves organized then, mate. Since you arrived, you haven't seen anybody—no guards, no other blokes?" O'Malley shook his head again. "I counted five of these cells . . ."

"There are five more on the other side."

"Go on? Names on the doors?"

"Yes."

"So we should soon be having company. You've taken a good look round?"

"Not all that much. I've slept most of the time. Bashing my head didn't help."

"Reckon there's a way out?" O'Malley shrugged. "It must be some sort of jail," went on Raxby, shaking his idea like a dog with a rag. "And there's always a way out."

"How do we know it's a jail?"

"You don't reckon it's a holiday camp? Of course it's a jail. I can smell it." Raxby sat there on O'Malley's bed, hugely pensive. "We must be violent types, you and me." He was still gnawing away at the inexplicable—a boy who, in his lost life, liked things simple. "Even the guards are scared of coming within sloshing distance. They just pickled our brains and shut us down here like rats in a trap." A new fear crossed his face. "I wonder what we done, O'Malley? And when do we get to meet the others? And the guards—there must be guards—the bastards can't leave us here to rot. They've got to bring our fodder, for a start."

"They don't bring it, they send it." O'Malley told him about the shaft.

"Yeah?" Total perplexity. "Any idea, yet, what sort of place this is?" O'Malley's clockwork brain teased at some fragment of past general knowledge. "The steps lead down to a crypt, I think."

"Jeez, a crypt! Isn't that where they used to bury people?"

O'Malley wasn't sure he liked Raxby. "Yes, but they were usually dead at the time."

At the shaft, Raxby poked his head under the stone face. "Could that be the way *we* come?"

The idea hadn't struck O'Malley before. "Hardly likely, is it? They put us to sleep first and there wouldn't be room to lie down."

"You can sleep sitting up," said Raxby. It sounded a piece of absurd irrelevance. "Not that I'm saying you haven't got a point. There must be other ways into this place—and ways out too. What's for breakfast?"

At first, O'Malley thought that everything was exactly as he'd left it. The bread was cold and a little stale. How much had he eaten? Not more than half of one of the small loaves—yet a piece had been broken off a second and not by Raxby, apparently.

O'Malley tried to count the apples but couldn't remember how many there had been. One thing was for sure, though—it hadn't been *his* hands which had rewrapped the butter and cheese so neatly, the paper at the ends twisted and the packages themselves replaced side by side in their cardboard box. And he was pretty sure that other containers had been opened—ones that he had not bothered with; extra items of clothing, spare flashlight batteries . . .

He didn't mention this at once to Raxby, who had grown morose and silent. "Is this all we get? How are we supposed to spread the bleeding butter?"

"With one of those wooden things."

"Why didn't they send down a knife? Afraid we'd cut our throats?"

O'Malley wasn't hungry. He watched Raxby sniff at the cheese, ignore the honey, then devour a hunk of buttered bread as large as his fist. Raxby squinted at the churn, raised the lid, smelt the contents and winced. Not bothering with a paper cup he grabbed the churn in his big hands and sipped noisily straight from it, then spat out, and made a coarse reference to camels.

"It's all they've given us to drink," said O'Malley. He suddenly didn't like the way Raxby glared back at him over the rim, the swarthy face brooding with some undeclared suspicion.

Raxby gulped at the milk again, spilling it down his chin. Then he gave O'Malley another of his shifty glances and said, "Let's sit around for a bit. We might catch ourselves a guard. The bleeders have got to show their faces some time."

"Not a chance," said O'Malley. "They obviously let this stuff down with a rope, and it's at least sixteen feet up to the top." Whatever he said to Raxby had, he decided, an uneasy ineptitude—a smugness he couldn't seem to avoid. And Raxby might be tough, but he was all jangling nerve ends and baffled resentment.

Suddenly O'Malley found six feet of solid fury towering above him. "You know it all, don't you, mate? What are you—a dirty little guard? Yeah, I got it—they planted you down here to watch me. I should have twigged it from the start. I may have lost my memory, but I'm not stupid. Come on, let's have it. Who am I? What am I doing here?"

An arm like a crane jib lifted O'Malley clean off the floor, swung him round, drove him against the wall. "The keys! Give me the keys. Christ, if you don't get me out of here right now, I'll spread you all over the stonework. Come on, you bastard—the keys!"

Then Raxby's fists were whirling, pummeling his stomach, aiming at his face—and O'Malley had no more will to resist than a rag doll.

He must have been out for seconds before he found himself crawling about on the cold stones, choking, retching, fighting for breath . . .

Then, just as suddenly, it was all over. Raxby was kneeling beside him, patting his cheek. The fires in his eyes had turned to ashes and his stained teeth were grimacing with contrition and self-disgust. "Sorry, mate. I don't know what come over me. If I ever do a thing like that again, clout me on the head with a hammer."

THE MORNING SPENT ITSELF GRUDGINGLY UPON THIS
strange prison and its inmates. It was miserly of clue, frugal
of hope. Yet sometimes a sound dropped like a copper coin
into a well . . . the distant lowing of a beast, the passing
song of a bird or the fidget of vermin.

Sunlight filtered parsimoniously through the small cell
windows, turning the walls into checkerboards of light and
dark—not that the light revealed much.

It stayed just bearably cold with a dank chill, which
seemed to belong to those stones. The chill penetrated
cloth and clung to bone—and yet when O'Malley, later on,
gave his tiny patch of sky a longing glance, he was sure that
this was summer.

But where?

They cleared the delivery platform, stacking the boxes
tidily near by. Raxby, affably churlish again, gave the vacant platform a sour look and a moody kick with his toe.

He glared up at the glass hatch: "Wonder when the shop
opens again. Some time tonight? If we could only catch
sight of their ugly faces, it'd be better than nothing. If and
when a few of the other blokes turn up, you know what I
reckon we could do? Stand on each other's shoulders, with
the one at the top waiting with a crowbar. I'll volunteer for

that bit any time. Meanwhile, instead of staying in our beds, we'd better keep our ears to the ground, mate, and find out how they bring us in. They can't do it by bleeding magic."

O'Malley said, "I've a hunch somebody else has already arrived." Raxby must have clouted him too hard—he'd clean forgotten noticing that the stores had been tampered with. He told Raxby now.

Raxby chewed at an apple. "In that case, he's keeping out of sight a long time, isn't he? We haven't even heard him kicking stools about yet! Poor sod—probably bawling his guts out in his cell, missing his mum. Reckon we'd better find him and put him out of his misery? It's a wonder he hasn't heard us clattering about."

"He may be in the other row. This place is pretty soundproof."

"Let's take a look."

The third cell along was as vacant as the others but bore evidence of a recent and meticulous occupation. The sleeping bag had been left unzipped, the flap folded back neatly, corner to corner. On the locker top, in a perfectly straight line, were a toothbrush, a tube of toothpaste, and a slightly damp tablet of soap.

"Where the hell's he got to?" grunted Raxby. "I never noticed the name on the door."

"Bainbridge . . ." O'Malley opened the locker. Most of the clothes as well as the sneakers and flashlight were missing. "He could have fallen down somewhere. Had an accident . . . those vaults are tricky."

"Where's my tin hat?" asked Raxby. "Better grab an extra light from one of them other cells."

O'Malley fetched it and they went down the nearest steps. It was a strange, higgledy-piggledy place as O'Malley remembered; arch after arch, tantalizing passageways that got you nowhere and always a cloying odor of putrefaction.

Their feet padded without resonance through the twists and turns, and sometimes they were forced to crawl, pawing through drifts of sterile dust and debris. Here and there their hands slithered across a moist patch of mildewed stone.

O'Malley tried to keep a mental check of the direction they had taken. Raxby seemed content to dog his heels, swearing when his big frame bruised itself on a projection and occasionally hanging back and probing hopefully at a loose stone. If he was dreaming of a way out, thought O'Malley, he was likely to be disappointed.

There was a sudden intersection and the choice of four ways. O'Malley paused at the hub, swinging his light beam.

Raxby slithered to his side. "Can't we do better than this, mate? I'm beginning to feel like a bleeding mole."

O'Malley called out, "Anybody there?"

Not even an echo at first. Then, at O'Malley's second shout, a casual response from not far ahead: "Hello, there!"

O'Malley picked his way toward the voice, light dancing like a firefly. By the time Raxby caught up, O'Malley was standing upright and playing his beam on a flight of narrow stone stairs. A figure was crouched up there on a tiny landing. Behind him was a large door, arched at the top, with stout iron bands bolted vertically to the panels.

The figure covered its eyes with one arm. "Go easy on the searchlight, old boy. You're searing my eyeballs."

O'Malley turned the beam away. Raxby said, "What the hell are you doing up there, mate?"

"Trying to pick the lock with a coffin nail or whatever it was I knelt on coming through the catacombs. Not a chance, of course. I'm Bainbridge—I think. Who are you?"

"O'Malley."

"Raxby."

The second light beamed dustily down the stairs, alighting briefly on each of them in turn. "Nice to meet a couple of fellow human beings. I was beginning to think I was the only one left in the whole damn universe. Some plague, perhaps, and myself the only survivor. Frightful scare, actually."

Bainbridge's cell enjoyed a few streaks of morning sunshine. It was warmer, now, with the strip of barred sky a hazy and untroubled blue.

Untroubled also seemed Bainbridge, lying relaxed on the bed, a long, slim youth of uncertain age, hands locked behind his neck. He had slightly protruding ears, brown hair cut shorter than theirs, long nose, a mouth that turned up at one corner when he smiled, and eyes that were disconcertingly direct.

Whatever trauma Bainbridge had suffered in his solitary awakening, he appeared to have himself, and this inexplicable situation, perfectly under control. He was relatively immaculate, too: it was Raxby and O'Malley who looked and felt like a couple of sewer rats.

And it had evidently taken only a short time for Bainbridge to size them up. "I did wonder, at first, if you were the Forces of Darkness. But when you emerged, like a couple of blind mice trying not to tread on a mouse trap, I thought: Bainbridge, old boy—or whoever you are—keep a grip. If they—that's you—were mental nurses in pursuit of a rampaging lunatic—that's me—you'd be wearing white coats and waving jolly old hypodermics. Conclusion—we're all in this together."

Raxby was bestraddling the stool, clicking his teeth and scratching his chin as Bainbridge drawled on. There was suspicion in his eyes, contempt twisting his ugly mouth—yet already something else in his bearlike stance, as if, thought O'Malley, he were trying to make up his mind whether the new arrival could possibly be as naïve as he sounded.

All Raxby said now was, "I suppose it's no use us asking when you got here and how?"

"Haven't got a clue, old boy. Some time during the night, I suppose. I woke up in this funny little room. Damn birds and their dawn chorus . . . they murdered sleep, as the Bard said. I must have lain here for half an hour biting my nails to the quick until I thought of trying the door. Never occurred to me that I wasn't a one-man show. The old brain box wasn't functioning, I suppose. Frightfully fuzzy. Well, once one had peed and that sort of thing, the most sensible idea seemed to be to shuffle around and try to find an emergency exit. I must say, I was hopeful about that door where you found me, but I might have known better. The damn thing would do credit to Alcatraz."

O'Malley asked, "You couldn't even see through the keyhole?"

"No, some blighter's stuffed it with chewing gum, I think."

Raxby picked his teeth. "Even if we can't bust through the bleeding thing, at least we can mount a guard. Now there are three of us we ought to be able to jump any guards who turn up."

Bainbridge tweaked his mouth. "*Guards*, old chap? But they don't have to be anything of the kind, do they? I mean, can we be sure that this is some sort of penal settlement? Nobody's given us short hair cuts. We haven't been made to trot at the double round a barrack square—even our cell doors aren't locked. All the options are wide open, old boy. We could just as easily have been kidnapped."

This was too much for Raxby. "Come again?"

"The Mafia might have robbed us," announced Bainbridge, closing his eyes. "At this very moment, perhaps, some thug with a handkerchief stuffed in his mouth is calling our families and telling them to leave large parcels of unnumbered bills in various telephone booths—or else. The Mafia knows about drugs, doesn't it? It would have been easy for them to pump us full of dope and then lock us up in this ruin while they wait for the showdown. Either that, or we've been carried off by little bug-eyed chaps in flying saucers. Everybody knows they've been skimming across the surface of the earth for centuries making a preliminary survey. They want samples of Homo Sapiens to carry back home—some obscure little planet just south of Andromeda. We'd be the last to know, of course. That would account for the awful plumbing in this place. I mean, we're in a space ship and they haven't got things quite right. The mock-up is meant to keep us happy."

Raxby's teeth grated. "Tell me something, mate. Do you ever stop talking?"

"I don't really remember, old boy!"

Unexpected seriousness came from Raxby—squatting on the stool like a chained bear, waiting to be fed. "I'll tell you something, mate. When I woke up, for a minute I thought I was dead."

Bainbridge gave him a long look, his eyes flicking briefly at O'Malley. "That, old boy, was because you'd forgotten your name. But there's a lot more to oneself than just a name. The blighters are clever, but they haven't really destroyed our identities. O'Malley is O'Malley. You are

Raxby. I am Bainbridge. Even if they got the labels mixed up on the doors, it wouldn't make any difference. We are still men, my lads! We are rational. We know true from false. I'll tell you something. When I woke up, I had the screamingly funny impression that I was a maggot curled up in an apple. Then I thought: come off it, Bainbridge, old boy, you're nothing of the kind. It's the world that's gone screaming off the rails, not you. Do you follow?"

Raxby shook his head. "It still don't make sense."

"Perhaps when the others have arrived, our captors will herd us together and give us chapter and verse. It could turn out that we're part of a stunt—a deal to take part in some soppy TV commercial having to do with goats' milk."

O'Malley broke in, "There's something puzzling me, which doesn't seem to have occurred to either of you. If we have been drugged, the effect won't last forever, will it? It'll have to be renewed."

"Yeah," agreed Raxby. "And to get me they'd have to send at least two blokes, one coming ahead with the tear gas and his mate bringing up the rear with a needle."

Bainbridge abruptly sat up. "There's one point we may be able to settle at once. Neither of you has noticed any punctures in his skin, I suppose?" He began unbuttoning his battledress blouse. More disconcertingly, he dropped his trousers. "Have a good look, O'Malley."

O'Malley shrank at first. Then he forced himself to examine Bainbridge—limbs, buttocks—and finally he shook his head. "No, nothing like that."

Bainbridge started to dress again. "So they probably didn't do it intravenously."

Raxby rolled his eyes, "Just my luck, getting locked up with a couple of bleeding intellectuals. Nobody's looking at *my* ass!"

O'Malley kept his sleeves buttoned.

Bainbridge lay on his bed again. O'Malley was beginning to think that it looked more like a throne every moment. "That leaves little white pills. I must say, they've done rather a good job on us. No clues. Nothing to help us remember. Clothes . . . nothing in the pockets, not even an old bus ticket. It's rather like having been born yesterday with our boots on."

Raxby took on the role of Court Jester. "Maybe we're prisoners of war. Any minute now the Gestapo is going to come frog-marching down them stairs and take us out and put us up against a bleeding wall." Then he took himself seriously again. "No, I still say this is a jail. What crime d'you reckon *you* committed, mate?" He was asking Bainbridge. It evidently mattered to him what Bainbridge thought.

Bainbridge opened his palms. "Oh, mass murder at least, old boy! Can't you see the blood on my hands?" He sat up. "Who's for lunch? We might as well raid the larder. No doubt our mysterious keepers will send us more."

For all their talk and pokings around, they learned nothing new that day. Even Raxby's scheme to keep watch on the door came to nothing; he was back in his cell asleep before sunset.

And O'Malley, gradually overtaken by a torpor he couldn't account for, crawled off to his bed earlier still.

5

THERE WERE THREE NEW ARRIVALS THE NEXT MORNING, crouched at the foot of the delivery shaft, foraging among a fresh cargo of boxes. It was Raxby who came across them, on his way to the washroom.

The boys' faces turned to him one by one—nobody moving until the threat in his approach could be determined. There was a thin youth with a parchmentlike skin; another, thicker set and a little taller, with a speckled pattern of freckles and healing sores, and a third boy, undersized, hair a straw-colored brush, nose pointing like a beak.

They each wore the drab denims and sneakers. Raxby hovered over them for a few seconds, widening his shoulders, "Don't guzzle all the food, There are three more of us, so far."

The small boy looked perky. "That all? What's this caper?" He meant the shaft.

Raxby didn't trouble to answer. Instead he asked, "Where are you lot from?"

The small boy said, "Bed!"

The freckled boy finally swallowed what was in his mouth. He asserted some kind of seniority, shooting glances at the others, then fixing his eyes on Raxby. "You shouldn't go creeping around, mate. We thought you was a guard. You might have got yourself clobbered."

"Don't get too ambitious," said Raxby. "Give us your names."

They had no idea yet what he represented. The small boy answered, "Skeel."

"Landers," said the one with the pale face.

"Hackett." His mouth was full again.

"That is, according to the names on our doors," said Skeel.

Hackett seemed to pick up some earlier argument. "What are you going on about now? Surely you know your own name, stupid."

Skeel ignored him. "Who's in charge down here, you?"

"Not particularly," shrugged Raxby. "There's a guy called Bainbridge. Bit of a twit, but he'll listen—if you've got problems, that is."

"He knows . . . ?" asked Skeel.

Hackett swung back at him. "What's there to know? I can't see no problem."

"You must be joking!" Skeel giggled, gulping his cup of milk.

Hackett helped himself to something more. From its wrapping it looked like cold sausage—that was a change. And he took another half a loaf of bread.

Raxby watched. "*You've* got a problem all right, mate. Where do you put it all?"

"What's it to you?"

Landers said, "We're wasting time. Where is this Bainbridge?" He had a very quiet voice: slow, unemphatic, oddly flat like the expression in his pale eyes.

"I'll see if I can find him," said Raxby. "Stick around."

"All I want to do is sleep," yawned Skeel.

"Stick around?" said Hackett. "For how long?"

Raxby grabbed a crust of bread and a slice of the sausage

meat, which Hackett had just sawn through with a spatula. He beat Hackett's hand to it then swaggered off, munching.

Bainbridge said, "We'd better call them in, then. Not all together—one at a time. Divide and rule, if you follow."

"Rule?" asked O'Malley.

"Sooner or later one of us has to take charge." There followed one of his odd pauses. "It doesn't have to be me, of course."

"I'm not pushing for president," said Raxby. "You're welcome, mate. Unless *you* fancy yourself a spellbinder, O'Malley?"

"No."

"Well, we don't have to be portentous about this," said Bainbridge. "I'll chair the meeting if you like, but don't be afraid to chip in when you want to."

"Some chair!" grinned Raxby at the prone Bainbridge. "They're going to ask some awkward questions, mate. Got any new answers?"

"I'll think of something."

"Well, skip the bug-eyed monster bit."

Bainbridge looked thoughtful. "What are they like—this new lot? Did you get their names?"

"Skeel, Hackett and . . . oh, yeah, Landers. They're just blokes. One was feeding his face, another acted like a kid at a circus. I don't fancy the third—Landers. I'll fetch the first one now."

Hackett came first. His face was red, his cheeks still bulging; he walked with a false swagger. "What are you all in for?"

"We're asking the questions, mate," said Raxby.

"Okay, okay. To save time, I'll give you a bit of my life story. I was running this gang, see?—before they caught up with us. We made a mint. Shops, fairgrounds, places like that. No violence—well, not much—but in the end a copper got his nose busted in. Not by me, it was one of my mob. I took the rap, though, being the leader, like." He glanced round, trying to discover what sort of impression he was making. "Crazy place this, isn't it? Where're the guards? Not that it's a bad jail—I've been in worse. You too?"

Nobody answered. Bainbridge said, "Well, we'll see you around, old chap. Give the groceries a miss on the way out. We all have to eat. Send one of the others in. Skeel will do."

Hackett seemed at home with orders. He nearly saluted. When he had gone, Raxby clicked his teeth. "Who's he trying to kid?"

"Himself," said O'Malley.

"Yeah, under the big act he's wetting his pants," said Raxby. "We could have put him out of his misery."

"Why should we do that, old boy?" asked Bainbridge. "He didn't strike me as being very bright. He's probably the sort of chap who can't stand too much reality. He'll come round to it, in his own time."

Skeel crept in, blinking. Bainbridge tried a trick question. "How old are you, Skeel?"

Skeel just shook his head. "I don't know, mate. You tell me! Hackett's stupid, trying to pretend. Did he tell you that yarn about going round in a gang and getting caught for beating up a cop? I bet it was the same fairy tale he told me and Landers." Then Skeel became pathetically anxious, "It isn't only me that's crazy, is it? Only . . . you lot have been here longer than us, so maybe you've made a few guesses. What's happened to us? When are they going to let us go home? What have we done?"

"We don't know, old chap."

O'Malley added. "We're working on it, Skeel."

Raxby saw the tears well up in Skeel's eyes and shuffled on Bainbridge's stool. "Don't suppose you done anything very bad, kid. Maybe you tried crawling into somebody's mailbox and got stuck!"

When Landers arrived he stood there like a pale ghost, clearly having no intention of listening to lectures, treating them all with a remote superiority and total lack of interest. "Look here," he said to the ceiling, "why are we all sitting around—doing nothing? We've got to get out." He appeared to be calm as a corpse—until suddenly his thin hands began to race over his body as if on the run. "For Christ's sake—we've *got* to get out."

Bainbridge surveyed him thoughtfully. "All in good time, old boy. And there's no point in going off half-cocked, is there? If we all go thrashing about, banging at the walls and things and acting provocatively, it'll probably only be the worse for us. Far better to keep cool, bide our time, lull our keepers into a false sense of security . . . until we know just who the enemy are."

Landers' voice was hardly above a whisper. "I'll find out!" He turned a short, misty gaze on them and vanished.

Bainbridge raised his eyebrows. "So much for our interrogations. Not a stunning success, eh?"

O'Malley said, "Landers might be useful—seems bright—but there's something about his eyes . . ."

"His eyes are what worry me," said Raxby.

Bainbridge said, "Oh, it's the drug surely. Yours, Raxby, aren't always jolly to look into either!"

But Raxby was uncompromising. "The bloke's a nut—it stands out a mile. That's all we need. And useful for what?" Something else—not only Landers—seemed to be bothering Raxby. "That guff you gave him, about not provoking the guards or trying to escape . . ."

"I didn't quite say that, but I rather thought we'd agreed . . ."

"I never agreed to nothing! And I don't remember O'Malley doing it, neither."

O'Malley looked uncomfortable. "The trouble is . . . we don't know what we're up against. On the whole, I go along with you, Bainbridge. Whoever they are, they've got the upper hand. They must have thought of everything we're likely to do. Every time we do something impetuous, we'll merely play into their hands. If we want to seize the initiative, we've got to be subtle."

"Amen, old chap," said Bainbridge, his face impassive.

Raxby chewed sullenly, bunching his big fists in that familiar gesture of barely controlled aggression. But for the moment he didn't labor the point. "I know what they're trying to do—bore us to death. There's nothing to do in this place. In a decent jail, you have television and football and all that. And if you got no better way of passing the time, you can always get a rise out of the guards. They even let you write letters home—if you got a home."

"How do you know all that?" asked O'Malley.

"All what?" Raxby thought it over. "I don't know, it just come out!" He noticed what he thought was suspicion in O'Malley's face. "What's eating you, mate?"

O'Malley flushed. "Nothing."

Bainbridge detected the edgy feeling that was so often between the other two. "You see, O'Malley, Raxby's little homily is rather like your remembering bits of the Catechism, as you once told us. It's even possible he's never been near a jail. Our minds are stacked with useless and misleading information. Whoever put us here and their nasty little pills have, in this sense, turned us into computers. Give a computer plenty of tape to punch and fit it with wheels, and it'll trundle its way happily along from London to Oxford. That doesn't mean it'll actually recall its journey."

Raxby didn't seem to be bothering to take all this in. "That chap Landers has a point. We ought to be planning an escape."

"Are you sure that's what you want, old boy?" asked Bainbridge.

There was a quick look from Raxby. "What's that supposed to mean? Of course, I'm sure. You think I want to spend the rest of my life stuck in this rat trap? Tonight, let's have a go at watching that door—if we can find some matchsticks to prop our eyes open with. There are four more blokes to be smuggled in."

Bainbridge considered. "We could lose an awful lot of sleep for nothing, Raxby. They probably don't use the door at all—it's a bit obvious. There may be more ways in and out of this place than Hampton Court Maze. It would be just like them to choose an open sesame we haven't cottoned on to yet."

"Okay," said Raxby. "So what about the shaft?"

"Not *that* again!" said O'Malley.

Raxby glared at him. "Look, it's simple. Apart from the locked door, the shaft is the only way in or out that we know. The guards have to open up every time they deliver the food, and somebody must be holding a rope at the other end. So we grab the rope, give it a quick jerk, and with luck the guard at the top won't have time to let go and we'll have him. A bit more luck and he'll pitch clean down the shaft and break his neck."

"And then what?" asked Bainbridge.

"At least we'll know if he's human or a bug-eyed monster from outer space."

Bainbridge said, "I suppose we could give it a try."

"Now you're talking sense!"

"On one condition—no violence. Observation only—a fact-finding mission, not a flagrant act of suicide. As O'Malley so sensibly put it, we don't know who we're up against. The Johnny holding the rope could be some kindly old watchman with arthritis and a ring full of keys in his baggy trousers. On the other hand, I, for one, don't much fancy getting my face blown off by a shot gun—or worse."

"I'll do it," said O'Malley. "If I can keep awake."

Raxby looked from O'Malley to Bainbridge's bed, then back to O'Malley. "And I'll come along, too. We can clout each other every time our heads nod."

"I'd rather you didn't, old boy," said Bainbridge.

"Don't worry, we'll do it your way. No violence—that what you said?"

"You may not be able to help yourself, Raxby."

"What the hell do you mean?"

Bainbridge didn't quite answer the question. "When it comes to Armageddon, we shall all be glad to have you around to prop up the barricade, old boy. Meanwhile, I'd prefer O'Malley to do it solo. One chap will be less conspicuous than two." It apparently didn't occur to him that Raxby would challenge him further. His eyes stayed closed as he went on, "Tonight, then, O'Malley, it'll be you. You'd better try to get some sleep first. And mind you don't get your skull cracked when they send the platform down." He glanced instinctively at his wrist. "I'd say let's synchronize our watches, only they don't seem to have invented time here yet."

Raxby snorted, already heading for the door. Bainbridge opened one eye and said, "If you're pushing off, old chap, buzz round to the others and issue a general directive, will you? Everyone keeps clear of the shaft tonight. Orders."

In O'Malley's cell the enigmatic rectangle of gray daylight deepened into an even more mysterious indigo.

He waited until he saw the first star, then rolled up his sleeping bag, and made his way alone to the shaft. He daren't climb into the bag but spread it double against the wall so that his body would, he hoped, be insulated from the cold stone.

He settled himself down in almost total darkness, knees drawn up, head bent forward, like an ancient, blindly waiting for some excavator to stumble upon his primitive grave.

He felt only slightly apprehensive and more than usually wide awake. Once or twice, early on, there was the whisper of footsteps some distance away; the flush of a toilet, the suggestion of a reflected flashlight beam.

But his alertness weakened and apathy returned as little weights pressed on his eyelids. He fell into a fitful sleep, then awoke, startled and guilty, his head humming with a half-remembered dream—he was buried in a hollow grave and somebody was moving his headstone . . .

But he knew it was the winch mechanism he'd heard. Groans, squeaks—as if the thing was straining with an almost intolerable load. Not a rope but a chain, unwinding with tortured protests from a drum.

O'Malley didn't use his light—yet. But he knew that, as soon as the platform had reached the end of its descent beyond the stone face, he must make a dash for the shaft and use the precious seconds while the hook was being detached to try and catch a glimpse of faces above.

The platform continued rumbling down. It paused for an instant as though snagged on something growing out of the stonework. Then on it came, swaying to and fro, bumping the stone walls on each side; got stuck again—and dropped the last foot with a shudder.

The chain rattled as it was jiggled free of the hook on the frame. Above, there was a faint, muffled, explosive sound as the glass hatch doors closed. Too quick!

Then, in the silence, O'Malley knew that the crude elevator had carried a different cargo: something *breathed* in front of him!

O'Malley was frozen out of movement. He found the flashlight switch with his thumb, plunged it on, and uttered an involuntary cry.

The figure in the wheelchair had its face turned toward him: a grotesque and awful face; eyes closed, head tilted to one side, teeth bared in an idiot grin.

And, dangling limply against the spokes of the big wheel, was a misshapen hand the color of white wax.

6

O'MALLEY SAT ON HIS BED WAITING FOR DAWN TO BREAK.
A different star winked in his window—a meaningless bea-
con sending out an incomprehensible message. Yet the
night's tide was on the ebb—O'Malley heard the first twit-
terings of birds, no louder than wind-blown trees across an
unknown landfall.

So he stuck it out—he wasn't going bleating to Bainbridge or Raxby yet.

He had dragged the wheelchair and its burden from the
platform and shoved them along the pitch black passage to
the washroom. No point in that, though—the automatic
light had gone out. He'd found his way back to his own cell
and pushed the chair in there.

The grotesquely tilted head slept on and O'Malley was
stuck with it, shivering with the cold and a residue of horror. Once he tried crawling in his sleeping bag, but how
could he sleep with *that?* So he shivered on, sometimes
squeezing the switch of the flashlight and playing the beam
over the chair, and only gradually did this become less of a
plunge into terror.

The upper body was wrapped in a thick gray blanket,
leaving the arms free. At the bottom, the blanket folds
tapered away to such an extent that O'Malley thought the

creature had no legs—until he saw the toes of sneakers poking out at the bottom and resting inertly on the step of the chair.

Nothing covered the face. It was not disfigured by damaged tissue although there was a puffiness about the skin—evidence of old and severe bruising, perhaps. All of the boy's features were grossly out of proportion: a great dome of brow formed a hood over a pair of large, sunken eyes; the nose was flat and one-sided. The mouth, with its broken teeth, hung open in a permanent leer, and there was an enormous jaw, shiny with the protuberance of underlying bone, resting stiffly at an angle on one shoulder as though grafted there by a devilish surgeon.

Which one of them was he? And why had they sent him? Another thought occurred to O'Malley. Suppose he hadn't been keeping watch on the shaft that night? How long would this bundle have huddled there at the bottom unattended?

Gradually O'Malley's window slit let in the new day and he no longer needed the flashlight, could no longer avoid the face. But now it had become familiar and somehow less repulsive. A life of sorts breathed from its mouth and nostrils and the ugliness mattered less.

Suddenly the figure opened its eyes. For a second an unexpectedly direct gaze chilled O'Malley to the marrow. Then the eyes rolled away, apparently trying to focus on things in the dim cell. The mouth moved, there was a grunt and a forming of froth on thick lips; then the boy placed both hands on the arms of the chair and began to whimper, eye-whites turned appealingly towards O'Malley.

O'Malley wanted to say something but didn't know what. He left the boy and groped his way to the shaft. At the little supply cache beside the empty platform, the milk churn was still a quarter full. O'Malley half filled a paper cup from it and carried it carefully back to his cell.

He couldn't have been gone more than three minutes, but in that time Bainbridge and Raxby had arrived. Bainbridge, hands in pockets, stood just inside the door, eyebrows raised at the wheelchair.

Raxby was squatting on the edge of O'Malley's bed, gnawing his thumb. "Blimey!" he said. "Now I've seen everything. The poor bastard looks like he's been put through a mangle. Where did you find him?"

Presumably the crippled boy didn't hear or understand: he was staring vacantly at the lightening window bars.

"They sent him down the shaft."

"Jeez!"

O'Malley placed a hand behind the boy's neck, raised the head, and tried tipping milk into the mouth. Most of it was spilled.

It was only then that he noticed a card tucked into the collar of his shirt. No pins. "Conway!"

Raxby said, "He was screaming. We thought it was you, being grilled by the Gestapo."

Bainbridge asked, "Did anything else happen?"

"Happen?"

"At the shaft, old boy, last night."

O'Malley laughed—a touch of hysteria in the tone. "You think *this* wasn't enough, Bainbridge? Anyway, no. It all happened so quickly—and it looks like we're going without breakfast this morning. It was as much as they could do to get *him* down, without bacon and eggs as well."

Bainbridge said, "I only asked because there are two other newcomers, snug in their beds. Raxby and I checked up. Wheeler on your side, Miller on mine—next to Conway's cell. We'd better push him round and settle him in.

By the way, you didn't hear the patter of tiny feet when the other two arrived?"

O'Malley shook his head. Raxby couldn't take his eyes from the wheelchair. "Bet they *was* brought in through that door."

"Possibly, old boy. Presumably it was only Conway who arrived by the lift—more convenient, I suppose, then bumping him down the steps."

Raxby gnawed his thumb again. "Reckon he can talk? And who's going to take care of him and that?"

"We'll work out something," said Bainbridge. "Take turns, perhaps. Now there are nine of us . . ."

"Full house, then?" said O'Malley.

"Not quite, old chap. You've forgotten Travers. Perhaps he missed the train."

Conway whimpered, Raxby scratched his chin. "Bleeding guards! Reckon it's their idea of a joke? I mean, if this place is a jail what's he doing here? What could *he* have done?—unless he tried to poison his nurse."

Bainbridge said lightly, "Perhaps he succeeded, old boy!"

It must be around noon, O'Malley decided; Bainbridge's barred window was a shimmering blue. The heat was becoming stifling, and Bainbridge, having called a meeting, told the last one in to leave the door ajar.

He, apparently, had no intention of relinquishing his bed, so apart from Raxby perched on the stool, the rest squatted or leaned, brushing and bumping against each other like sheep in a pen. Conway, asleep again, was parked in one corner beside Miller.

Together, the slight oddity and alienation they shared was more marked, their faces pallid and vacant with half-

identify. Something—something forgotten?—had blanked their eyes if not entirely dulled their wits. They had the shocked, abandoned air of orphanage waifs.

The two new arrivals, apart from Conway, were trying to pick up clues. They had only their nervous glances in common. Miller, plump and short and several years the younger, had a tuft of corn-colored hair and a round, choir boy's face: often his lips quivered and he had a mannerism of putting both hands to his mouth and nibbling at the nails.

Wheeler was taller and much darker; lean hips animal-taut, long fingers clenching and unclenching; narrow brow, thin lips, small ears. His eyes sometimes changed to white pinpoints.

Bainbridge crooked his fingers behind his neck and, as if it required considerable physical effort, let his eyes drift around the circle of faces. "I've called us together just to put everybody in the picture—though, as most of you realize, there isn't one, really. Some person or persons unknown has seen fit to drug us to the eyeballs and dump us in this jolly old hole and let us stew for a bit. It's rather mind-bending, I admit, but there doesn't seem to be much we can do about it for the moment except to stay calm. The whole show probably hinges on a johnny called Travers. According to the names on the doors, he's due to complete the team—then things may start popping.

"Now about the food, such as it is. Go easy with it. The guards, or whatever they are, appear to be starting a new branch of Weight-Watchers. We had better have a rationing system. The Committee—that's O'Malley, Raxby and myself—will store the food here and dish it out. By the way, there's only goats' milk to drink. Not every chap's idea of an elixir, but probably full of vitamins—so take a good swig several times a day. Any comments so far?"

None yet. Conway gazed, glassily awake now. Hackett guiltily stared at the domed ceiling, Wheeler's scowl was still in place. Miller's lower lip quivered, Landers' cheek twitched.

Bainbridge went on, staccato: "Showers every day—there's plenty of soap. And don't leave food in your cells—there may be rats about. And fitness. If this goes on much longer, we don't want to turn into cabbages. We'll organize something—a little jogging, perhaps. Take it easy with your flashlight batteries. There are spares, but our mysterious hosts are hardly likely to brighten up this place like Piccadilly Circus. Anything else?"

"Recreation," said O'Malley.

"Yes, one really would have thought they might have supplied us with a few table games, scrabble. . . . Ah, well. Nobody appears to have taught them how to run a rummage sale!"

Bainbridge turned serious again. "Escape. In case any of you are bursting with wild ideas, I'll run over one or two things we've already discussed and dismissed. Windows—forget them. They're difficult to reach and the bars—both in the cells and the washroom—appear to be constructed of high tensile steel. Unless the goons obligingly pop us down a supergrade hacksaw, wrapped up in a set of spare underclothing, nobody's going to saw through those bars. However, if anyone gets a brainwave come and see us—the Committee. Don't try to go it alone. If there *are* goons, they may be a little crazy, but I don't think they're stupid—and there is a difference."

Landers said. "That door."

"Tried it," said Bainbridge.

"What with?" Landers sounded calm, rational.

"A rusty nail, old boy."

"Huh! What about a tunnel?"

"Come again?" Bainbridge flickered his eyelashes. "Oh, you mean like the Count of Monte Cristo—through solid stone? I can't remember the story very clearly, but I rather think it took him several years. We're hoping we won't have that long."

Skeel put in. "Might be other ways out—somewhere in them arches. I been looking. I can get in small places."

"Keep at it," smiled Bainbridge. "But report back to the Escape Committee."

Then Wheeler asked, "This Committee . . . who rigged it up—you?" He was quizzing Bainbridge.

Bainbridge raised himself on one elbow. For a moment their eyes locked, both expressions remote, as if they were trying to recognize one another through a thinning mist. "If you fancy yourself as leader, old boy . . ."

Raxby slid from the stool and loomed over Wheeler. "Something bothering you, mate?"

Wheeler's hand snaked into a pocket, instinctively feeling for a weapon. "Who are you—Al Capone?"

Raxby said, "Could be, for all I know! Watch it!"

They might have come to blows, only suddenly Conway's loose mouth hung open and he began to gurgle, then scream with a long, drawn-out secret agony.

And something broke Miller. Without warning, he covered his face with his hands and went berserk.

He tore about the cell, temporarily blind and mad, hitting the walls full on, bouncing back; then, like a demented moth, trying to find the door.

Hackett made a grab for him. Then Landers, then

O'Malley. But finally it was Raxby who got hold of his clothing and hauled him aloft. "Take it easy, kid." Clawing away the hands, he slapped Miller in the face, to and fro, to and fro.

Very slowly, Miller sank to his knees—then cried. He cried softly and naturally, like a small child. Raxby breathed hard, buried his fingers in Miller's fair hair and ruffled it.

Bainbridge watched for a while. Then he said, "At this point we might adjourn the meeting. I rather think Conway wants the toilet. O'Malley, be a good chap and wheel him along to the washroom. Perhaps you could persuade Miller to go with you."

7

THE WINCH MUST HAVE LET DOWN THE DAY'S SUPPLIES during Bainbridge's meeting. Because of the heat, Bainbridge modified his storage plan and had everything perishable stacked against the cool passage wall immediately opposite his door. It was impossible to set a fixed time for meals, but at reasonably judged intervals everyone could be rallied to collect their share.

The only novel items, apart from an additional churn of milk, were a special drinking cup—presumably for Conway—and several packets of chewing gum. O'Malley rifled through it all and said, "Nothing labeled—not even the chewing gum. What's their secret?"

"Home cooking, old boy," said Bainbridge. "And perhaps the gum was manufactured in Tottenham and they don't want us to know that the factory is within range of their horse and buggy."

O'Malley said, "It's funny about words. I suppose it comes from not having anything to read down here. Even 'Not Fit for Drinking' is becoming like a poem."

On their last trip back to the shaft, Bainbridge, O'Malley, and Raxby found Hackett. Not pilfering for once.

He was standing there, naked except for gray briefs, on the lift platform, body filthy with reddish dust, sweat streaming out of every pore in the green liquid glare of the glass hatch. He seemed pleased to have an audience. "Say, watch this!"

He started to climb, fingers and toes clawing at the stonework, miraculously finding little holes in the rough surface. He was going up with his feet splayed against the shaft walls. Within seconds he was perched like a shiny green angel with his abundance of gingery hair practically touching the glass at the top. "Easy!" he said.

"Bleeding marvelous!" said Raxby, chewing incredulously.

Bits of loose mortar and dust spattered down the shaft as Hackett descended, eventually taking a grip of the platform bars with bare, prehensile toes.

"What do you think?" Hackett's deceptively clownish face was triumphant.

"Mere words cannot express it, old boy," said Bainbridge.

"All we need," said Raxby, "is a chunk of rock to bash the glass in with. There's probably a beam on the other side that Hackett could shift."

O'Malley said, "Of course, we don't know what—or who—is on the other side of the hatch."

"No," agreed Bainbridge, noncommittally. "Rather a pity if Hackett got through only to find the goons sitting round a table playing rummy."

"It must be out in the open," said Raxby. "Look at the sun. And Hackett would have the advantage of surprise— better than us clattering about trying to make a ladder. All he'd have to do is wind the winch down and up we'd go— taking on any goons we meet."

O'Malley asked, "What about Conway?"

"Haul him up on the lift, of course. Anyway, some of us could make it."

Bainbridge studied his face, "You seem to have it all worked out, Raxby. Do I take it that you knew Hackett was going to try this stunt?"

Raxby grinned. "Well, he did just happen to mention it—in the john."

Bainbridge said, "What do you think, O'Malley?"

"Yes . . . it's too good a chance to miss."

Hackett watched each of their faces in turn, anxiously awaiting a verdict.

Long, careful deliberation from Bainbridge. "Right ho," he said at last. "After dark, of course. We'd better work out a contingency plan. If we're going to storm the jolly old Bastille, we don't want to botch it. One failure and the goons will probably cut us off without a crust. But not a word about this till I say so, Hackett. We don't want a flap—we'll delay any announcement as long as possible."

Like a little act of providence, Skeel emerged from the catacombs. He would have done credit to any early Victorian chimney sweep; his hair alone would have doubled as the brush. His much rubbed eyes resembled those of a startled panda.

Skeel placed a number of objects on Bainbridge's bed, a panda pup waiting for a pat on the head. "Any use?"

A metal spike, slightly rusty and pitted, of totally unknown origin. It was eight inches long, one end tapered to a blunt point. There was also a four-inch fragment of a pickaxe or mattock with a scraping edge.

"Where did you find all this, old chap?"

"Just lying around—in different places," shrugged Skeel, vaguely. "You haven't seen nothing yet, though."

He dragged from his pocket the head of a venerable, antique hammer. It had a claw for extracting nails, and there was still a stump of rotting wood stuck into the hole.

"How's that?" beamed Skeel. "Please, can I have a new battery for my flashlight?"

Bainbridge still hadn't called a meeting to discuss Hackett's escape plan when Raxby and O'Malley came across Landers in the passage near the washroom.

He was stripped down to his undershirt, staring up at some point high on the inner wall. Very enrapt, he was juggling a piece of flint in one hand, brow furrowed: he looked even thinner and more fragile without his denim top.

"Have you ever noticed those pipes?" he asked.

There were two, side by side, close together. They were painted a nondescript white, protruded from a point just below the slightly curved ceiling, were bracketed to the wall at several points, and then vanished into the stone floor.

Raxby and O'Malley couldn't see what he was trying to tell them. Landers said, "Will one of you go into the washroom and turn on all the taps for a few seconds? You might flush one of the toilets as well."

O'Malley obliged. There was a rush of water followed by the flush of a cistern. Landers stuck a finger in one ear and pressed the other hard against the pipes.

O'Malley turned off the taps and came back. Landers said, "I thought so. These pipes are duds. There's no flow in them at all." He suddenly seemed to treat their presence as an irrelevance, as if they had merely broken into some train of thought.

"The water supply must have come from the mains at

some time, but it's been bypassed since. That accounts for the comparatively low pressure—and the disinfectant, of course. I wonder why they did that? They connected the washroom to a reservoir tank—perhaps a water tower. Yes . . . it would take quite a lot of gravity to build up enough pressure for all those outlets, and if there was any sort of pump near by, we'd have heard it. I suppose somebody climbs up a ladder with a bucket of carbolic and tips it in. I *wonder why?* Not just for hygiene surely . . . rather crude." Landers' voice had begun to die away in private speculation.

He crouched to his knees and began carefully tapping the floor with his little stone. The light was rather dim down there so he fished out his flashlight and traced the beam along the cracks and began tapping again. "Hear the difference?" When Raxby and O'Malley shook their heads, he addressed them in a slow, deliberate voice as if explaining some simple principle to a pair of retarded infants. "Solid here . . ." he tapped the floor. "But quite hollow— *here.*" More taps. "My guess is that there's some sort of conduit underneath the stones. The mortar's different, too. When they rerouted the water supply, the stones must have been removed and cemented back. Neat job. And did you know that wall you're leaning on is a boundary? I've been working it out. Pretty thick, of course, but if the conduit goes underneath the foundations . . ."

So that was it. Landers was on his tunnel kick—and today, of all days!

He suddenly abandoned his little stone hammer and sat back against the wall, folding his arms. He gave them a ghostly smile. "I suppose you've realized by now that this place is . . . ecclesiastical?"

Raxby chewed. "So we're under Canterbury Cathedral!"

But Landers was looking at O'Malley, eyes enigmatic and slightly wet. Then a thin hand vanished into his pocket. "What do you make of this, O'Malley?"

Lying on his palm was a plain wooden cross, no more than two inches long. O'Malley took it, handled it, turned it over. No inscription, a very hard, lightish brown wood. Simple, perfect in shape, a tiny hole pierced in the top.

O'Malley asked, "Where on earth did you find it?"

"On the floor, just inside the washroom. Easy to miss it—it was tucked round the corner. I only noticed it because I was tracing the pipes. I don't think it's been there long, though—no dust, no stains." His face broke into one of his pale distant smiles. "Can I have it back?"

He still gave Raxby the creeps.

Everybody was present—eyes fixed on Hackett, nerves taut as they'd been all through that long, untimed interval since Bainbridge's last meeting. The pockets of their full denim uniforms were bulging with stones, their only weapons; Bainbridge had taken charge of the ugly metal spike Skeel had discovered.

Hackett stood at the foot of the shaft, top clothes tied round his neck leaving his limbs free. Raxby handed him the pick blade and hammerhead, wrapped into folded cardboard. "Stuff it in your pants and don't drop it."

"Hell, it weighs a ton!" Hackett looked happy, though.

"The elastic should hold it. If not, we'll have to try chucking the pieces up at you when you're on that ledge."

Hackett, face piratical in the green moonlight, took the pick blade out and jammed it into his mouth.

"Good luck, mate," said Raxby.

"Hear, hear!" added Bainbridge.

Hackett scrambled on to the platform frame and began his climb.

Once his feet were out of range, half a dozen heads poked under the shaft face, watching Hackett's sure progress.

Unmeasured seconds ticked by and then . . . a hoarse, stifled yell from above. The clink of falling metal was followed swiftly by the more frightening descent of a body.

Hackett's! He was bent painfully over the frame, his face contorted in multiple flashlight beams. Nothing was broken, it seemed, but his hands and arms were coated with a thick, viscous sludge.

Raxby was first to make an impromptu chemical analysis. "Oil—bleeding engine oil!"

Hackett nodded, fighting for breath. "Smeared all over the wall, near the top. A snake couldn't crawl up there no more."

Faces were stunned, eyes bitter with disappointment and questioning.

Raxby played spokesman. "The bleeding goons done that. We're stuck down here now, like wasps in a jam pot. How come? I'll tell you. The goons knew what we was planning. And I'll tell you something else. We've got an informer down here. One of us is talking to the goons—don't ask me how."

8

EARLY AND ALONE TO THE WASHROOM NEXT MORNING, O'Malley was coming away from a stall when a faint figure crossed the periphery of his vision—like a furtive pursuer trying to outflank him. Only his reflection in the mirror, of course!

He brooded again upon a recent suspicion—or was it pure fantasy? The trouble was, he thought, ruefully, how could you tell the difference—when selfhood was but a ghost and real so unreal?

But suppose Raxby was wrong?

Having nowhere else to congregate unless Bainbridge called a meeting, they'd all tended to use the washroom as a club—hanging about, chatting as freely as they ever did, and it was here that Hackett had "lobbied" Raxby, wanting Bainbridge's assent to his attempt on the shaft.

The looking glass could be their informer! Someone watching and listening . . . a one-way mirror, with microphones attached. The first time he'd thought of it, one of those scraps of knowledge, attached to no personal association, had flickered automatically in O'Malley's brain: they used such things in institutions—mental hospitals, places like that. One side was an ordinary looking glass, the other a window.

What lay behind the washroom wall? A secret room? It was impossible to tell, and the mirror itself, though O'Malley hadn't dared tamper with it, seemed to be cemented into the wall with four large bolts.

He dried his hands at last, caught sight of his dark reflection again, and instinctively moved away. Should he mention his suspicions to Bainbridge and Raxby?

He wished he hadn't bothered! Raxby and Bainbridge were companionably facetious.

"Can find out easy enough," smirked Raxby. "Toss a brick at it."

"That'd be rather drastic, old boy," said Bainbridge. "Suppose there's a harmless little goon sitting on the other side with a notebook on his knee? Or Tweedledum and Tweedledee. But I really can't see O'Malley as Alice Through the Looking Glass, can you?"

O'Malley looked at his feet. "I thought of putting Landers on to it. If there's a space behind, he'll find out. He's making a sort of map, did you know?"

"Ah, Landers, the idea man," yawned Bainbridge. "Tell him what you like, old boy. But at the moment he's got a thing about his tunnel, chipping away like the reincarnation of a hyperactive stone age man."

"Yeah," said Raxby. "I lent him them tools Skeel found."

Bainbridge's tone changed. "You might have mentioned it before, old chap. I'm not trying to push rank, but I'd like to know what's going on. It's the responsibility of the Committee to plan and coordinate escape projects."

O'Malley said, "Perhaps we ought to have Landers on the Committee."

"Hell, no!" said Raxby.

Bainbridge thought: Make us rather top heavy, wouldn't it? What was it some chap said about committees?

They meet to design a horse and finish up with a camel. And Landers prefers to do his own thing, like young Skeel. Better just to pick his brains—and watch that he doesn't overreach himself.

Landers, in fact, had more than one string to his bow. This morning it was the big door at the top of the crypt steps. He knelt in the darkness, playing his light beam on the formidable keyhole.

Not for Landers those vain, ill-considered jabbings with implements. He had brought along the bits of tools, but for the time being they lay unused beside him. The light beam, throwing a reflected glow on his face, made his eyes shine, disclosing the intelligence that lay beyond the mists of drug or sickness.

There was the thinnest sliver of daylight beneath the door but none through the keyhole. Either the key had been left in the door on the other side or, more likely, there was a hinged cover over the aperture. Why that side and not this? No answer, no data. Not important. But the daylight and the draught on his hand at the bottom indicated open space.

Landers wanted the space. "Don't you see?" he had asked. "We've *got* to get out." But with intelligence, not blind force. Or that idiot, Hackett, doing monkey tricks!

The key aperture became, for Landers, a Black Hole into a different universe. He had taken the lens from the spare flashlight—Travers'—and now he used it as a magnifying glass. Yes, there were scratches on the metal surrounding the keyhole. Bainbridge or somebody poking about with a rusty nail? Or did the faint circular pattern indicate the recent use of a *key?*

The metal spike was useless as yet—too thick and

straight. With the claw hammer, he'd wrenched free one of the links from his bedspring and managed to bend the tip into an angle. Landers probed, carefully. Useless! It wouldn't turn those massive tumblers. And there was no gap in the lintel wide enough to use the mattock blade as a lever.

But he had his other idea. He should have waited—waited till the sun was up.

Later, then. Landers collected his bits and pieces and had a thought about the door: had they all made oblivious journeys through here, like bodies pushed into a crematorium?

Then, quite unawares, his vision came again. It was always between sleeping and waking. As he shone his light down the stairs, they were suddenly dissolved in flames. Why *this* strange and terrifying fantasy? Why *flames?* Why was he stumbling, choking through fire—as if a phoenix of identity stirred in the ashes of his memory? He returned to his cell.

The sun burned high now—and it worked almost at once: the lens of the flashlight focusing into a star-bright pin point, producing the first curl of smoke.

Very early that morning, Landers had collected stones and, moving his bed well out of reach, built a little fireplace in the center of his cell. For a chimney he'd climbed up and smashed the glass in his window, sensing the immanence of an unknown countryside aromatic with ripening corn, softly whispering with the muted industry of wild life.

Now he was watching the first tiny flame tongue the shredded paper, then grow and grow until the fire had a new-born voice. It crackled and licked at the underlayer of stouter material—carefully arranged strips of cardboard.

Only when he was sure the little fire's infancy would not now be stifled did he lay across the top slivers of soft wood he had chopped from the door of his locker, using the mattock blade.

When the fire glowed red hot, he carefully pushed in the metal spike. He had prepared a crude anvil of two stones with the claw hammerhead waiting beside it. His purpose was to shape the metal spike into a finer point and bend it at an angle—making a more efficient tool with which to tackle the lock of the big door.

And yet . . . it was as though, with a double forgetting, his mind had temporarily lost hold of its plan. The flames in themselves were *all*, forming pictures which were akin to waking nightmares. Some revelation was being writ large in those leaping flames, but the time had not come yet when Landers should read it.

Any concealed observer, watching through a one-way mirror in the washroom, would have had an excellent view of Wheeler's profile as he leaned against a basin, talking to Hackett.

Sinews rippled beneath his undershirt, too long denied their violence; he had a soft-footed young panther's stance but a sallow human face beginning to alter its contours with a growth of black beard. His eyes, bright in the centers, were preying upon Hackett—big, stupid-looking Hackett—munching discontentedly at his hunk of bread and washing it down with sips of milk.

Miller squeaked in with Conway's chair, making for one of the stalls.

Wheeler said, "He can wait. Stick him in the doorway, sideways on. We don't want to be interrupted—sudden like. You can listen if you want, Miller—might do you a bit

| 69 |

of good. Only keep one ear open and tip us off if Bainbridge or any of his lot come this way."

Miller looked resentful but obeyed. He had developed an unexpected talent for Conway's supervision which no one discouraged, and his concern for the well-being of his charge didn't include using him as a prop for one of Wheeler's shady conspiracies.

Wheeler's eyes went back to Hackett. Hackett was turning something over in his mind—something Wheeler had just said—and Wheeler was letting it sink in. Hackett took a slow bite from an apple, let its flesh roll about in his mouth.

Hell, Wheeler was thinking, the bloke was thick—thick as a wall, but feed him the right bait and he'd be hooked. The other kid—Miller—didn't count, much less that blubbering wreck he pushed around the place. But if you wanted friends you couldn't be too choosey.

Hackett said, "Oh, give over, Wheeler. It can't be like that."

"Don't be so dumb, Hackett. If you was here first and had a head start on everybody else, wouldn't *you* take what chances was going and look after Number One?"

"Maybe, but there are three of them."

"I can count," sneered Wheeler. "But they arrived more or less together didn't they? And we've got a squealer down here. Savvy? Maybe more than one. The fancy boy— Bainbridge—sets himself up as mouthpiece. He's got the gift of the gab, I'll give him that. And he's got that gorilla, Raxby, as strong-arm and O'Malley for yes-man. What do we know about any of them?"

He let Hackett think. Hackett said. "Well, that goes for the rest of us, don't it?"

"There's a subtle difference, mate," Wheeler said. "They

had time to learn a few things we never knew. Take the food, for instance."

Hackett stopped chewing. "What about the food?"

"You don't reckon that muck is all the guards send down, do you? We're just dished out the leftovers, mate."

"If I thought that . . ."

"Suppose they found out who the guards were, and in exchange for keeping their mouths shut they was promised something. Remission of sentence for good conduct say. And look what happened to you in the shaft."

"It was the goons done that."

"Who do you reckon tipped them off? Goldilocks? If you'd busted your neck, Hackett, I bet they'd just have laughed like hyenas."

Hackett's brain was ticking. "I still don't get it. I mean, even if they was getting extra food and special privileges, why would they want to stay in this hole if there was a chance of escape?"

"You're thick, Hackett! Who said they was staying? Who's the escape committee? *Them.* And why do you think they're stashing away all the best food?" Wheeler laughed.

Hackett was half afraid, half infected. He began to laugh too. "You're a case, Wheeler!"

"Can't you see, mate? They're going to ditch us. They won't be taking you nowhere, Hackett, nor me, neither." He looked across at Miller. Miller saw his eyes, and his mouth trembled. He grasped Conway's push handle in tight fists. "And they won't be taking you out, Millie—nor 'im, poor bleeder. Unless we all stick together, like."

Wheeler broke off as footsteps approached the washroom. It was only Skeel, so Miller let him through. Skeel was carrying something in his arms, something wriggling to free itself. "Look what I found—a cat! Blimey, he give me a turn—he was just wandering about down in the dark. When I saw his eyes, I thought he was a ghost."

Miller suddenly broke into giggles. Skeel's joke, Skeel's face, the black cat scratching and spitting in his arms—these things stirred some infantile merriment in him. Miller's moods were extreme. He giggled until tears sprang in his eyes.

Hackett caught it. He guffawed, smacked Miller on the back. Conway flinched.

And Wheeler's laughter was manic, if contrived: "A cat! Fancy a cat. . . ." The three of them were drunk with laughter.

Skeel blinked, not understanding. "Hey, what's funny? You're frightening my cat!" But even he grinned.

Hackett bellowed, "Say, Wheeler. If the cat got in, it must be able to get out. It can show us a way out!"

"You're not a cat," said Skeel, and it might have been the funniest remark he'd ever uttered.

"Let's go and look, Hackett," said Wheeler. "Let's all go and look. Put the cat down, kid, and boot its rear—give it a good start, like. We'll follow it and see where it goes. Right, Hackett?"

"Yeah," chortled Hackett.

"Hold on!" said Skeel. But he put the squirming cat down. It scuttled through the doorway, fur bristling, and darted straight for the vault steps. Wheeler and Hackett were plunging after it. "You'll lose me cat," said Skeel. "And I've only just found him!"

He heard Miller, still giggling, squeaking Connie into a stall—but he didn't wait. He was already far behind Wheeler, Hackett, and the cat.

Wheeler had a flashlight. Skeel beamed in on it, threading through the familiar vaults, his own light dim. The laughter ahead sounded eerie and mad.

Then Skeel knew they had stopped. Their flashlight was playing hide-and-seek amid the dank arches. He nearly caught up.

"There the cat goes," said Wheeler. "Up the steps, back to the passage."

"I can smell smoke," said Hackett.

"What smoke? You're thick, Hackett!"

"Smoke, I tell you!"

"Maybe the cat has lit a cigarette!"

More inane laughter.

Skeel reached the steps. He heard Connie's chair squeak along the passage behind him. He was sure the others had caught the cat by now. He thought he heard it squeal, but perhaps it was only Conway.

Skeel followed.

The noise was totally inexplicable and, even more alarming than the first sniff of smoke were those curling wraiths from beneath Landers' door. Bainbridge, with Raxby and O'Malley behind him, put his hand around the latch.

The fire in the center of the room flickered at their intrusion. At first nobody noticed their arrival except perhaps Conway, slouched in his wheelchair in one corner, eye whites turned to the opened door.

They had formed a human snake and were encircling the fire, Wheeler in the lead, then Hackett groping at his hips, then Miller. Last of all came Skeel clutching a cat under one arm.

The four of them were shouting the last snatches of an idiot song. They were stamping their feet, twisting their bodies, faces contorted, eyes rolling.

| 73 |

As their chant came to an end, they broke away from the circle and made dances of their own, leaping about the cell, beating their arms like wings.

Wheeler was shouting, "Who's giving us toast for breakfast and hot soup for supper?"

"Landers!"

"And who's going to burn the place down and let us out?"

"Landers!"

"Landers *who?*"

"Landers the fire-maker!"

Landers stood apart, face ash-white and uncomprehending. Then he saw Bainbridge. The others followed his gaze and all action froze.

Bainbridge had taken one step into the cell, and his eyes were locked into Wheeler's. Wheeler stared back with that strange pin-point of half-recognition then, without a word, picked up a sock someone had discarded. Wrapping it about his hand, he dived straight at the fire and there was a weapon in his hands.

The metal spike glowed red hot and it was pointing straight at Bainbridge's throat.

Wheeler came on, step by step, eyes as bright as flames.

Bainbridge knew this was no charade: Wheeler's mocking triumph held the soullessness of a natural killer.

Raxby tried to push his way in but found himself elbowed back. The terrible dagger was losing some of its luminosity, but it was quite close enough now for Bainbridge to feel the heat of it on his face. He waited perfectly still, hands in pockets.

He waited almost too long. The tip of the spike was an inch from his throat when his hands shot out and were suddenly steel clamps on Wheeler; one on the deadly wrist, the other at his neck.

A miraculous half-second and the spike spun harmlessly away, and Wheeler's entire body was revolving in midair before thudding to the floor. Bainbridge was on him at once—knee in the groin, one hand pinning him down by his hair, two splayed finger tops resting firmly on his cheeks just below the eyes.

Bainbridge said, "If you ever try a thing like that again, old boy, I'll break your bloody back!"

The secret room was equipped with an archaic field telephone. To make contact you had to lift the heavy handset and whirl a handle almost as big as that of a sewing machine.

You waited . . . and waited. If the Abbot himself wasn't available, one of the other monks would promise to deliver a message.

This time it was Father Ignatius in person; remote, patient, sympathetic, sometimes exasperatingly ironic and infuriatingly detached. "So you feel they may be suffering from side effects. But my son, what are *they* but side effects—Society's side effects. The little fire dance you describe doesn't strike me as much more than a prank. Boys will be boys, as we used to say. However, I agree that Wheeler's behavior was . . . disappointing." Pause for thought. "You are keeping up their sedation? You could try increasing the dosage."

"Very well, Father."

"And in the circumstances perhaps we should move straight to Phase Two. You can arrange it?"

"I think so."

"Excellent! Our prayers go with you, my son."

Thanks! "Bainbridge" thought. Something tells me I'm going to need them. He replaced the handset and yawned. He faintly resented this night work—having to keep his eyelids propped open until the early hours, when everyone else was safely and enviably asleep, before daring to creep away to this place.

Still, there was a consolation: as often as not the monks probably had to get Father Ignatius out of bed or interrupt him at Vespers! That would explain why he sometimes sounded rattled.

Perhaps, from now on, things would be easier—though he would still have to keep up his act. Bainbridge fished in his denims for the large key he'd kept there, guarded like the way through St. Peter's gate. He sat staring at it for some moments, working out the simplest method of putting it within someone's reach. Young Skeel's, perhaps?

Then he left, locking the little room behind him.

9

BAINBRIDGE WAITED. MEANWHILE, OVERRIDING RAXBY'S objections, he wangled Landers onto the Committee. Things had quieted down since the fire dance, but it would be wise to keep Landers unobtrusively under his eye and away from Wheeler.

When, after "breakfast" the next morning, Skeel turned up, there was a not unfamiliar expression on his dirty face: a mixture of quirky triumph and Cockney caginess.

He fished something new out of his pocket and tossed it onto Bainbridge's bed. It was a large key of unusual design which Bainbridge immediately threw to Landers.

Skeel said, "Couldn't miss it. Found it at the bottom of them steps, the ones with the door at the top."

Bainbridge was watching Landers' face. "What do you make of it, old boy?"

Landers studied it through his flashlight lens. "I'd say it had been used recently. It *could* fit the door."

Raxby slid off the stool. "Only way to find out."

O'Malley frowned. "It can't be that simple. It's all . . . too convenient."

Bainbridge tickled Skeel's cat. "Yes . . . unless that tame goon of ours—the one who dropped the cross in the washroom—has been even more unspeakably careless. Lead the way, Landers, only softly, softly. No point in getting the other chaps steamed up until we're sure. You can come along, Skeel."

"Oh, thanks. I was just thinking I ought to put my cat out!"

On the stone staircase Landers' long, thin legs might have been mounting a scaffold. At the top he stared for a long time at the key in the crisscross of torch beams. "Stick her in, mate," said Raxby, impatiently. "What are you waiting for?"

The heavy lock responded at once. Landers hesitated again, then slowly pulled on the ring. The door swung smoothly back so that, crowded too close on the landing, they had to retreat to be clear of its arc.

A blaze of sunshine struck their faces. Raxby blinked, poked his head through, and gasped: "Blimey—Wembley stadium!"

They were standing on the warm flagstones of a covered cloister walk; heavily arched, bound on four sides by the fronts of stone buildings. In the center was a grass quadrangle. It was dry and uncut with, here and there, patches of rusty brown. But after their confinement it was like rich pasture land. They could smell it—for what seemed a long time they drank in the very breath it breathed, their nostrils tingling.

Skeel put the cat down. It raced at once across the quadrangle, sat in the middle, licked itself, then made a more sedate trek across to the opposite cloisters.

At last Bainbridge asked, "Where are we, O'Malley?"

"It's a monastery isn't it? Looks as if it's been deserted for ages."

Raxby brought himself back to earth. "That suits me,

mate. I was standing here waiting for machine guns to open up!"

Skeel said, "Nice to see the sky again."

Landers asked, "Monastery?"

O'Malley nodded. "But probably turned into something else . . ."

Their eyes, half blind still, moved nervously over the strange contours. No one . . . or no one yet visible. Suddenly Bainbridge laughed softly. "Good lord! I'll bet you're on the right track, O'Malley. Could this have been a school? Down below—those little toilets for little bottoms and tiny basins in which to wash filthy little hands. I rather fancy I went to a place like this once. My prep school—some establishment in Bucks, or somewhere, with a name like St. Trinians. It's all coming back to me—I can practically hear the ghostly whacking of canes. I wonder how many times the little Bainbridge crossed a quad just like this on his way to execution in the Headmaster's study?"

Skeel suddenly ran after the cat. He caught it halfway across, but instead of gathering it up and making a dash back for the cloisters, he stayed out there, doing cartwheels, then sat in the overlong grass, laughing, shouting, waving.

Raxby glanced anxiously up. "Stupid little twit! He'll be making daisy chains next." He ran out, grabbed Skeel—cat and all—under one massive arm and carried him back.

On the way his eyes swept the monastery roof. He noticed a feature none of them had yet seen—but at first his dazzled eyes didn't take in its significance.

The buildings had an air of abandonment and desecration. Windows boarded up or bricked in, the few that remained having splinters of glass held in place by cobwebs.

Their exploration of complex recesses and stone arches produced two ways in but, apparently, none out. For the present, however, curiosity was enough—and still no jailer emerged to challenge or deter them.

It was Raxby who found their first point of entry: a pair of curved doors with huge ring latch handles and no surviving locks. He kicked one open in expectancy.

A large, derelict chapel: a few twisted and broken pews, an altar covered with dust, the once highly polished rail still there, wobbling on its supports. The wall behind displayed a long rectangular shadow, suggesting, perhaps, that an altar piece had once been fixed there but long since removed. Beneath the high, heavily timbered and pillared roof were all that was left of the windows—thick wooden planks with an occasional flash of colored glass.

Bainbridge watched as they poked about, kicking at broken furniture, looking up at the roof. Only Landers seemed interested in the sanctuary. Hell! trust Landers to go door hunting, behind the remains of the choir stalls, then look down at his feet, stroke that ridiculous beard of his, brain sifting at something just short of suspicion. The dust . . . a scuffle of footprints. How clear were they? How suggestive?

Relax, Bainbridge, old boy! He said, "Nothing here. Let's push on, shall we?"

The room O'Malley found was on the other side of the quad. Furnished, after a fashion: faded carpet on the floor, a couple of armchairs, several others with torn leather seats. Along one wall were bookshelves crammed with volumes.

The smell of old polish still lingered. There was a small kneehole desk beneath a dangling light bulb. No switch anywhere: was it connected to the automatic timing device used for the washroom? The window was barred, of course. Landers drew up a chair and sat at the desk, blew dust from the top and began rifling through the drawers. They clacked open one by one and suddenly, with no change of expression, he held up a stub of sharpened pencil he'd discovered.

Skeel sprawled delightedly in one of the armchairs, cuddling his cat, dangling his legs, "Home away from home, isn't it?"

"Staff common room," nodded Bainbridge. "Make a change for the chaps—quite cosy, really. Somewhere we can spend our evenings, if that light works. I suggest we give the chapel a miss—bound to be rather drafty even on balmy nights. Not that they ever believed in giving the English schoolboy too much warmth—it led to bad habits. And books! We can all catch up on our interrupted education. Now, what have we here?"

He and O'Malley were running eyes and fingers along the mildewed spines. Bainbridge picked out a heavy book and flicked over the pages. "Encyclopaedia Britannica nineteen-twelve edition. Good lord, I wonder what they'll think of next? Some Johnny's just invented an airship. Fancies he could fly across the Atlantic, poor fool. What've you got O'Malley?"

O'Malley furtively closed his book, smile diffident. "Medical reference—there's a chapter on drugs."

"Oh, really? Have they come across aspirin yet?"

Landers had found a locked drawer. He was down on his knees, picking at it with his sharpened spike. He got it open without much trouble and laid the contents in a row on the desk.

A catapult with worn-out elastic; a paper bag of hard

candy welded together in one sugary lump; an old fash-
ioned mother-of-pearl comb; and a ship matchbox containing the fossilized remains of what might have been a cock-
roach.

"Behold, I bring treasures," said Bainbridge. "Ancient
confiscations, of course. An acquisitive lot, schoolmasters."

Raxby was tapping at a venerable wireless loudspeaker
fixed to the wall. No trace of attached wires. Bainbridge
made a routine quip about the young Marconi having been
thrashed here.

Raxby's euphoria was wearing off. "Right, we've had our
fun. What about some action? The way you lot are going
on, you'd think we'd never got through that door. Why not
have a shot at skimming up on the roof before the goons
wake up?"

Landers uttered one of his rare, unnerving laughs. "Do
you mean you haven't *seen* it?"

"Seen what?" But Raxby suddenly knew.

Landers, hysteria haunting his eyes again, stammered,
"They planted the key—don't you understand? They're not
letting us escape. Whatever we do, they're watching us."

Skeel's mouth dropped open. O'Malley sought Bainbridge's eyes but read nothing in them. Landers was off
through the door, knowing they would all follow.

They stood in the quad, shielding their eyes, looking up
and around at the roofs. Jutting out from every inch of wall
at topmost gutter height was a square-meshed grid. So far
as they could tell, it projected six feet or more from the
roofs, supported on powerful brackets. "Cunning bastards!"
grunted Raxby.

O'Malley laughed. "So we *are* in a cage!"

They went back to the walk, moving in a bunch, hugging
the cloister walls like little children who thought that by

hiding their faces their entire bodies would be out of view. Bainbridge hung back, waiting.

Eventually, Landers found a point where they could climb up, part way. It was at one corner where one of the stone posts supporting the cloister roof was chipped and defaced enough to offer hand and foot holds.

But it was Raxby who climbed up, O'Malley pushing at his feet. Raxby got a purchase on the cloister roof and worked himself along the tiles. O'Malley followed, then Bainbridge.

Landers and Skeel seemed content to watch.

They made a chain of outstretched legs and sprawling hands and then, with little chance of climbing further, the three of them were standing with their backs to the monastery wall at the top of the slope.

The grid was only a few feet above them now but out of reach. Necks twisted, they had a better view of its formidable structure—and, what even Landers hadn't noticed before, the interlacing of strands of barbed wire.

Raxby watched a sparrow alight on the mesh. "Reckon Hackett could make it?"

"I've no doubt he'll try, old boy," said Bainbridge.

The opposite walls still barred their view of the outer world, but it was possible to make out one or two new features: a belfry jutting its domed head above the chapel roof; the tip of a water tower, separate from the sprawl of building.

And, rising majestically on the far side, enjoying a commanding position, a crenellated tower.

Bainbridge saw a flash of glass catching the sun's rays. It twinkled twice, three times like a day star, then was gone. He didn't think either Raxby or O'Malley had noticed it.

Raxby, bearded jaw jutting up at the grid, was, no

doubt, clinging to a fading dream of early escape. O'Malley was looking slightly seasick. Bainbridge said, "If we stay up here much longer, we shall turn into gargoyles."

They climbed and slithered down, joining Landers, Skeel and cat. Disheartened footsteps plodded back to the door heavy with the false promise of freedom, which had betrayed and mocked them.

"We'll call a meeting and make some kind of announcement," said Bainbridge. He thought it in character to add: "Mustn't get everybody too excited, though. This little paradise is an improvement on our regulation eighty cubic feet of living space. We may as well enjoy it while it lasts. If we *weren't* intended to find that key, we can expect the goons to swoop at any moment—especially if everybody goes cavorting across the quad like a lot of giggling school girls playing hockey. What?"

Father Ignatius came on the line the next day: "Congratulations on Phase Two, my son. Everybody happy?"

"Wheeler's the main problem, still. His latest pastime is tormenting the life out of Miller. He gets at him through Conway, of course—grabbing his wheel chair and shoving it across the quad out of control."

"Ah, Wheeler. We must bear in mind the parable of the wheat and the chaff, my son! By the way, if on some future occasion your judo is not quite up to coping with a fresh outbreak of violence, we might authorize a means of securing your personal safety. A little tear gas, perhaps. But I'm sure you can manage Wheeler. You know him well enough. Does he like chewing gum?"

"Yes."

"Well, see that he gets more than his fair share! And doctor his milk as much as possible. Anything else?"

"We're finding the food rather monotonous, Father. And the spatulas break too easily."

The Abbot tut-tutted. "No knives, my son. The Home Office was adamant on the point. And we have a very limited budget . . . I'll see what I can do, though. I've been trying to persuade Brother Ambrose to part with one of his chickens. By the way, speaking of Brother Ambrose, he appears to have mislaid his cross."

"Yes, Landers found it."

Exasperated tone: "I've already had occasion to reprimand Brother Ambrose about those unauthorized nocturnal wanderings! And poor Landers . . . do maintain the utmost vigilance. His ingenuity could prove embarrassing. No more fires, and if I were you I'd find some means of confiscating those implements—unless he's under your immediate supervision."

Bainbridge ventured, "We have a lot of time on our hands; that's partly the trouble. Any chance of a few games for the chaps to amuse themselves with?"

"*Games*, my son?" said Father Ignatius, as though Bainbridge had made an improper suggestion. "I think we should tread carefully, there. As you know, one of the objects of this experiment is to discourage the lads from becoming too institutionalized. Most of them have had far too much ping-pong as it is. For the sake of their future rehabilitation, get them to use their initiative. And it is time to direct their energies toward Phase Three. Essential, as you know, that we motivate them to 'escape,' so to speak. For instance, give Landers every assistance with his tunnel. But be careful—the surveyor's report on the condition of the foundations was not altogether reassuring. As to a little harmless entertainment, Brother Benedict has been working on a device. It should have operated before, but he encountered a technical hitch. Keep up the good work, my son. By the way, have any of the lads the faintest idea where they are, yet?"

"A concentration camp!"

A throaty chuckle crackled along the wire. "And we are the *goons*? Well, well. *Achtung*, my son!"

Sometimes Bainbridge had an almost neurotic fear that he would get his phials and concoctions disastrously mixed up.

Doctoring the milk churns had proved simple enough, although he'd sometimes had to employ a certain sleight of hand. And the drug he used, though tasteless and harmless, affected people differently. Too much tranquility could jeopardize the project!—and of course the amount of milk consumed by each "patient" varied enormously, as did individual reactions to the tranquilizer.

This largely accounted for the sudden ups and downs of mood, the bursts of energy alternating with periods of slothful lassitude.

The chewing gum had caught on, of course. It was becoming a currency in the place—that was dangerous. He'd have to watch out that nobody died of sleeping sickness! But at least it meant that there was now one less potion to slip into the milk. On the first day he'd felt like a Borgia!

Conway was a minor problem—he didn't chew gum— but he seemed to sleep well enough. Perhaps Miller sang him lullabys . . .

Funny about Miller and Conway. *They'd* been right about them, right about Wheeler, too.

The earlier treatment—the *big* one, the experimental amnesia drug the Home Office chemists called Compound Y—apparently left some residue of half memory so that just as Wheeler still hated *him,* Miller's bond with Conway had not loosened its tragic hold.

Listening carefully at the sacristy door before emerging, the young man called Bainbridge thought: To hell with it! All you can do is your best, old boy! If they'd wanted a nurse or a chemist down here, they should have picked one—not a half-baked, underpaid social worker, a dogsbody, masquerading as Bainbridge of the upper classes!

But the Home Office, and this tiny band of Brothers they'd hired to do their leg work, knew what they were doing.

He hoped!

ON THE FIRST OCCASION THAT MUSIC EMANATED FROM THE wireless speaker on the common room wall, the immediate effect could scarcely have been more profound had the Archangel Gabriel himself stepped out of it.

Once the novelty had worn off, however, the incessantly funereal chords became an unswitchoffable bore. "Bleeding row!" grumbled Raxby. "Say, Landers, if you found the wires and connected them to the light switch, reckon the goon up there would get his hands burnt off?"

"Not if his apparatus was properly earthed," said Landers seriously.

Bainbridge set himself up as something of an authority. "Mahler, I fancy. Rather to be preferred to that Russian choir we had groaning at us all day yesterday. It just goes to show what an unspeakable chore it must have been, pushing a rowboat down the River Volga."

Landers was trying to count the hours, using a weird sun dial affair he'd constructed out of bits and pieces and erected in the middle of the quad. Impossible to be accurate, of course, with no chronometer to set up his calibrations—but Bainbridge, who had a watch concealed in his communications room, secretly marveled at how close Landers often came. Give him time! At this rate he'd find some ingenious method of plotting their position—with a cardboard sextant, perhaps; and the intricate plan of the monastery he was working on, scratching away with his precious stub of pencil, was sometimes worrying.

So was Hackett, hanging about in the chapel trying to find a way up to the roof!

Other activities mushroomed, as if their new-found "freedom" had begun to enlarge their spirits. O'Malley, borrowing the pencil from a reluctant Landers, drew a series of strange, abstract sketches—skillful and eye-catching—which he immediately gave away to first comers who stuck them to their cell walls with chewing gum.

Bainbridge made them a checker board with cardboard draughtsmen.

Wheeler went Bainbridge one better and, rubbing a bit of wood on stone until it was a rough cube, made it into a die. The stakes were strips of chewing gum. Wheeler, crouched in a corner and spitting on his hands, soon got to know which penciled number would most frequently come up—the cube wasn't accurately balanced—and anybody who played him was a sucker.

With private glee, Bainbridge watched Wheeler snatch his winnings, smirking like a croupier at a crooked casino, and was as relieved as Miller when Wheeler slunk off to his cell to sleep off his ill-gotten gains.

Still that extended patch of blue sky revealed nothing but birds and an occasional flash of glass from the lookout tower. Surely, thought Bainbridge, someone else had seen it by now? But if so, nobody seemed to have thought of it as having a human origin.

But one twilight there was a brief sensation. A few of the boys were out in the quad desultorily playing football with a rapidly disintegrating box of underclothes. Suddenly a helicopter clattered immediately overhead, navigation lights blinking. The boys waved and shouted. The figure next to the pilot leaned out against his harness and waved back—then the helicopter was gone, fluttering like an unheeding dragonfly across the tower.

Bainbridge watched the others' dejected faces and decided to step up Phase Three.

Meeting of the Escape Committee. Still no Travers, so Bainbridge had taken over his cell as Committee room.

The boys' beards had grown—stamping a new individuality on their faces. Raxby's was a startling black effulgence, Bainbridge's a humbler, faintly comic sprout; Landers' weak on the tip of his sharp chin, a querulous tuft bobbing up and down when he spoke.

O'Malley, digging at something with a spatula out of a plastic jar, resembled a tramp resting by the wayside. Yogurt! The Abbot's latest offering, sent down on the squeaking winch in response to Bainbridge's complaint. Doped? Probably not—except perhaps with a mild bromide to stop them from having Naughty Thoughts!

Raxby, moody, was suddenly half antitunnel. "I never said I was against digging a tunnel. Did I say that? All I'm saying is, don't be surprised at what you find at the end of it. It could be anywhere, from Margate beach to a salt mine in Siberia. So we've got this gimmick pretending we're in a concentration camp, but we're not, are we? At least those blokes knew where they was. They knew the goons an' all—they could give them cigarettes and chat with them, treat them like human beings. And they could see the machine guns on the walls, and searchlights and all that stuff. They knew what they was up against. We don't. We don't even know our bleeding selves. We don't know why

| 90 |

we're here or what we done. We've got no past—why should we fancy we've got a future?"

"But we've got a *now*, old boy," said Bainbridge, patiently. "It's what we do with *that* that matters. You know, sometimes Raxby you can be a bit of a wet rag."

"Thanks a lot! By the way, how are we going to get Conny out—build him a set of tram lines?"

Bainbridge stirred on Travers' bed. "Sometimes I wonder if we're not being honest with ourselves. Do we *want* to escape? And, at the bottom of our hearts, are we really keen to remember our pasts?"

"Of course . . . we want the truth," put in O'Malley.

"Sure of that, old chap? We've got to face it, you know. The truth isn't necessarily going to provide us with passports to the Bahamas—it may not make us free, as the Good Book puts it. The evidence, such as it is, isn't too reassuring—quite the contrary. We are all probably absolute pariahs, with an outsize debt to pay to society. In the eighteenth century—supposing this isn't the eighteenth century—perhaps we'd all have been swung on the ends of ropes to the applause of the populace." He opened one eye at Raxby. "Is that what you're afraid of, old boy?"

Raxby bristled. "Who said I was afraid?" He gave Bainbridge's question a lot of thought, then made up his mind. "Yeah, I want to know who I am and what I done. Don't we all?" Self-conscious, his hands kept on the move. "We got a right . . . what else was we born for?"

Bainbridge looked thoughtfully at him for a moment before he said. "So it's Operation Tunnel. When can we start, Landers?"

Now it was Landers' turn to look unsure. "Quite soon, I think. There's a certain amount of preliminary work to do first. I'd rather do it alone."

So, it appeared, would Hackett who hadn't yet got round to consulting the Escape Committee. He had preliminary work to do, too. That evening he at last managed to scale one of the chapel pillars and was clinging precariously to a rafter, groping with his bare feet for the ledge under a boarded-up window.

There was a slight diversion—Hackett had company. A minute or two ago a bird had found its way in through some chink that Hackett envied and was now fluttering along the ledge, squawking as it banged itself against the spider's web rafters.

White, Hackett saw. A pigeon—he was no ornithologist, but everyone knew a pigeon when they saw it.

Then, for Hackett, the chapel became positively crowded. Skeel had wandered in for some reason, perhaps looking for his cat, and his upward gaze was transfixed, sharing the bird's agony.

Still clinging, Hackett stared down at Skeel. "I think it's on its way down, kid. Try grabbing it."

The pigeon evidently thought a pair of outstretched human hands were as convenient a perch as any. Skeel caught it and held it. "It's got a ring on its foot."

Hackett had a couple of undershirts knotted round the pillar. He slipped into position and came down as smooth and skillful as a lumber jack. He put his shoes on and said, "It's a pigeon, right?"

"A racer, I reckon."

"Busted its wings or anything?"

"I don't think so. A bit dazed that's all."

"A pigeon," said Hackett. "They're supposed to home somewhere, aren't they?"

"Yeah, he must have been on his way home," said Skeel. "How did he get in?"

"Wish I knew!" said Hackett. "I've been trying to shift one of them planks. Not a hope, though. Still, if you're a pigeon you don't need much of a hole."

"Nice pigeon," said Skeel.

"You'll have to watch out for your cat."

Skeel nodded. "I'll take this out on the quad and let it go. It'll find its way home."

"Hold on!" said Hackett. "Not so fast. That pigeon could be useful."

"What for?"

"Pigeons can carry messages, can't they? Especially racers."

Skeel didn't see much in the idea. "I think I'll just let it go. It's got a right to its freedom."

"Haven't we all?" Hackett laughed. "Look, shove it in a box and cart it along to Bainbridge. Bainbridge ought to know we've found it."

Skeel didn't like doing it, but he found an empty box downstairs by the delivery shaft. He banged a few rough holes in it. Then he put in a blob of cheese and a few crumbs he'd swept up with his hand—that was all he could find.

Skeel, still minus cat, was present by courtesy at the meeting of the Escape Committee.

Raxby did his wet rag thing again, "Okay, so we got ourselves a pigeon and Landers has a pencil and we can write a message and pin it to the bird's leg. So what? What message? 'Having a spiffing time, wish you was here—we don't know where'?"

"I vote it's worth a try," said O'Malley.

Bainbridge thought quickly. "Yes . . . in the morning."

"Why not now?" asked O'Malley.

"Getting dark, old boy. And the bird does look a bit battered. It could do with a night's rest, and we haven't even composed the message yet."

"I'll look after the pigeon," said Skeel, enthusiastically. "He can sleep with me, in my cell. Can my cat stay in here, just for tonight?"

Raxby enquired, "Who do we address the message to? The Home Secretary? Reckon he'll send a parachute battalion to come and rescue us? I don't see why. After all, the chances are he was the one who plunked us down here in the first place.

Father Ignatius sounded slightly querulous. "*What* message, my son?"

"Oh . . . I managed to keep it fairly vague. I can't remember the exact wording."

"Most unwise! A careless communication falling into the wrong hands could prove an embarrassment to the entire project. I think it would be better to put the poor creature out of its misery. Humanely, of course. I'll leave it to you." He chuckled to lighten Bainbridge's burden as executioner. "I believe pigeons are edible, are they not?"

Bainbridge closed the cell door softly behind him, listened to the tranquil breathing from Skeel's bed, then shone a pencil beam of flashlight on the box at the foot.

The white pigeon had not had the benefit of a sedative and was rustlingly awake. When Bainbridge carefully raised the flap lid, a single red eye, bright as a ruby, stared warily, and the bird began to coo in mild apprehension.

Bainbridge got both hands right in, wryly despising himself because he couldn't bring them to take a strangle hold on the pigeon's neck. It would have felt like choking the life out of Skeel.

He closed the box and crept away, thinking: Not much of a hatchet man, are you Bainbridge, old boy? Who do you think you are—Saint Francis?

A full house turned out on the quad early next morning for the launching. Skeel held the pigeon, arms outstretched, lips pursed with concentration.

"Right—off he goes, kid," said Hackett.

Skeel let go, but the white pigeon seemed reluctant to give itself to the sky. It fluttered down at once and then, like an oversized white thrush rooting for worms, set off across the grass on foot, the rhythmical jerk of its head seemingly attached by a clockwork mechanism to the strut of its legs. Then just before it reached the far cloisters it took off, crash-landed, took off again.

"*Must* have broken a wing," said O'Malley.

As if it had overheard O'Malley and taken the remark as some sort of insult, the pigeon flew higher, then higher still, until it was a spotless white speck against the shadows of the monastery wall.

It would have to fly away from the cloisters eventually, away from that overhanging grid. It seemed to realize this itself, for presently, suddenly graceful and strong-winged, it peeled away from the wall and headed back across the green.

Then, from the observation tower somebody opened fire!

The whining bullets arrived a second before the crackling reverberations of gunshots. One crack, a second, a third . . .

Now' high above their heads, the pigeon began to

disgorge feathers as if in libation. Another flash from the tower, and another. For a second or two the pigeon darted swiftly across the sky, unable to make up its mind which way to go, how to fly off beneath and over the grid. Then the shedding of feathers became a shower, snowing slowly over the quad. And, a few strides away, there was a sudden small, sickening thump of a dead carcass and a splash like red paint.

Skeel cried out and ran toward it. Raxby was after him at once, catching him, sticking out a large foot, sending the smaller boy sprawling.

Then he bent over Skeel, picked him up, tucked him under his arm and carried him back to the cloister walk.

"BASTARDS!" SAID RAXBY, TOWERING GLUMLY ON TRAV-
ers' stool. "Okay, so it was only a pigeon this time. But
there're a couple of things we've learned. One, they're
armed. Two, any of us making a break out can expect an
assful of lead."

The cell was so dark that they had to track back through
the day to assure themselves that this was not nightfall but
early afternoon. And Landers' sundial was awash.

Heavy rain and wind beat against the window and sometimes there was a roll of thunder that shook the solid walls,
followed by searing lightning that exposed their faces.

Landers sat in a corner, thin knees drawn up, juggling
small stones in his nervous hands. "I hope that doesn't
mean we're going to give up."

Bainbridge kept his seething thoughts to himself. It had
been a stupid, mean little atrocity. Not just the pigeon—
they got shot every day in thousands. Not only that the
bird had been, briefly, a sort of naive symbol—a Noah's
dove sent out from their stone-walled ark in search of land.

No, it wasn't those things, nor even young Skeel's puck-
ish face when he'd seen the splash of red on green: the bru-
tal melodrama had affected Bainbridge for reasons of his

own. He was losing his grip, maybe, getting too involved. And losing whatever trust he'd had in the Project? All because someone had taken a pot shot at a pigeon? No— something else accounted for this sudden sense of being on shifting ground. A phrase he'd heard at College came into his mind: "There are the sane, the insane—and those who look after the insane."

Not altogether appropriate—until he gave his attention to Landers. "Give up, old chap? Certainly not. Tell us what you've found. Your scheme is first on the agenda."

Landers waited until the latest thunder roll had subsided. "I managed to dig up a couple of flag stones in the passage—where the water pipes are, you know? I put them back again, roughly, in case someone tripped over them in the dark. These stones are from the foundations. They're in such an advanced stage of erosion that you can pick them to bits with your fingers—I didn't have to use the mattock."

It could be tedious listening to Landers, but if you tried to hurry him, his eyes would turn as misty as amethysts. "I was right about the conduit, only it runs parallel to the wall. The pipes appear to go along the side of the building, not out at right angles as I'd hoped."

"No deal then?" asked Raxby.

"Not necessarily. It's the wall on the other side of the pipes which is crumbling. Look, I'll show you." Landers produced one of the bits of white card he always carried and the rapidly diminishing stub of pencil. He put a cross here, an arrow there. "Here's the route taken by the pipes and here's the conduit wall. It took about five minutes to pick a hole clean through it. There's a space on the other side."

"Any light showing through?" enquired O'Malley.

"No. But I thought I felt a draught of air. Of course, at

that level, even if it is the boundary wall, we'd still be several feet below ground."

O'Malley said, "Secret passage? I'm not sure this place goes back to the Dark Ages, but sometimes the monks had ingenious means of avoiding persecution."

"Ah, Attila the Hun," said Bainbridge. "Or are we in the wrong country?" He was back in character again. "How long do you think it will take, Landers, to gnaw enough of that wall away to get through?"

Landers pondered, eyes shining. "A day or two—if we work in shifts. Later, we'll probably have to dig our way out, somehow."

"We'll take turns then," said Bainbridge. "Now, what about Hackett's proposed death dive through the chapel roof? He thinks he can shift some tiles."

"Solo job," said Raxby. "Anyway, you can count me out—especially with that trigger-happy goon in the tower."

Bainbridge said, "I shouldn't think Hackett need worry. The chapel is miles away by comparison with the quad and from the crack of that nasty little firearm I'd say it was a point two-two. One of the goons probably uses it to shoot rabbits—that would account for the awful cold stew they sent down the hatch this morning. At that range, with a toy like that, they couldn't hit Westminster Abbey, let alone Hackett sprinting across some cabbage patch."

Raxby growled. "Okay, but Hackett's still got to climb down the pitch of that roof. If it happens to be raining, it'll be as slippery as a sloping ice rink. And how does he take off without shooting into space, maybe fifty feet from the ground? Of course, being Hackett, he'll expect to find a nice convenient drain pipe. Then I suppose he strolls off whistling through some cornfield with his hands in his pockets and catches a number nine bus."

"When is he making his break—assuming we give him the go-ahead?" asked Bainbridge. "You're the one he confides in, Raxby."

"Who, Hackett? You gotta be joking, mate. He wouldn't confide in his own little finger. He doesn't seem in any particular hurry—it's just one of his crazy ideas." Raxby gnawed at his thumb. "They'll know he's coming, of course—like they found out he was going to shin up the shaft."

O'Malley said impatiently, "Oh, give up, Raxby. You don't still think we've got an informer? Don't you think we'd have nailed him by now? There're only eight of us, unless you think Conway sends Morse signals from his wheel chair."

Raxby still enjoyed goading O'Malley. "Who was it who dreamed up that one-way mirror idea?" O'Malley flushed. "Only Landers found out it was an outside wall. I still say a squealer could do it. Somebody talking to that goon who creeps about at night, or writing him little messages he can pick up on his way to the john."

Landers suddenly realized Raxby's eyes were on the pencil stub and his little beard waggled indignantly. "I hope you're not suggesting it's me, Raxby."

"Oh, no. You're little Snow White!"

O'Malley said, "We know now that they post a lookout on the tower. He must have binoculars."

"And X-ray eyes and all?"

"He could put two and two together. He must have spotted Skeel's pigeon, for instance, and guessed what we were trying to do. And when Hackett did a dummy run up the shaft, the goons heard him and were ready for his second attempt."

Bainbridge kept his eyes closed and his tongue in his cheek. Good old O'Malley—perhaps they should have given this job to him!

The rain beat on. Bainbridge said, "Well, let's get back to Hackett and his plunge over Niagara Falls, shall we? Raxby's right, he'll have to go it alone. He's the only one who knows the Indian rope trick. When the time comes we must make it clear that he's only being let out on condition he fetches the cavalry, not just to whizz off to the movies."

Bainbridge was on the carpet.

"My son, I really must insist that in future my instructions are carried out in full—and without question."

"Yes, Father."

"We are all, of course, answerable to the Home Office. I shall hope, in due time, to be able to put in a highly commendatory report on your behalf. Won't do your future career any harm, will it?"

"No—thanks."

"This attempt of young Hackett's to get through the chapel roof . . . did you know he'd succeeded?"

"He hasn't escaped?"

Father Ignatius chuckled. "Good gracious, no! Surely you would have noticed if he had. I mean, he's lifted several tiles—and put them back again. Brother Jeremy was watching through his glasses. Food for thought, eh? And Hackett could have made it—the route down is perfectly safe and quite easy for a lad with his talents. Do you see, my son?"

"He doesn't *want* to escape?"

"Well done! You obviously have more acumen than the young man they sent from the Home Office to discuss security arrangements. I'm afraid he didn't follow my argument at all when I ventured to suggest that, just as these lads crave punishment rather than forgiveness, so they prefer captivity to freedom. Why else, as a purely secondary and passing phase of our long and arduous program, should we—at least in some cases—have to indulge in these elaborate contrivances? Try to work on Hackett a little. In case he should change his mind, we have Brother David standing by in the copse. But I'm afraid he'll find his vigil a little tedious. How is the tunnel proceeding? By the way, we have a small problem there."

"It isn't a way out after all?"

"Not in the terrestrial sense?" said the Abbot, obscurely. "However, Brother Francis is studying the plans. He may be able to tinker with the substructure beyond the vault. Meanwhile, there's a door in the east cloisters which it may be worth one of the lads investigating shortly. Tricky, though, my son—you'd better contrive to be present if you can. About young Skeel . . ."

"Skeel, Father?"

"Yes, do keep an eye on him."

"That isn't easy!"

"What *is,* my son? It may be wise to place some limit to his wanderings. A temporary shortage of spare batteries, perhaps. That cat he found . . ."

"Yes?"

"It isn't ours. Brother Bruce's is a Siamese. I sometimes feel that where a cat can go, young Skeel could almost follow! And Phase Three must remain strictly under our control."

"Yes, of course."

"I'll leave the matter in your excellent hands. What about Raxby?"

"Raxby, Father?"

"According to your reports, he seems to have become more and more apathetic. Ginger him up! Excellent material, Raxby."

12

THE SUN WAS BACK, TURNING THE QUAD INTO A STEAM
bath. O'Malley and Raxby worked their tunnel shift.
Landers spent his off-duty times repairing his "navigation"
equipment. Wheeler gambled in the cloisters. Conway
pushed himself in his chair, Miller sometimes having to
trot to keep up. Skeel was missing again.

Raxby, stripped to the waist, eventually threw the mattock blade down and said he needed some fresh air. So
O'Malley was alone.

He had a headache, a hum in his ears and spells of dizziness. The stifling heat, he supposed—and the unpleasantly
stale drift of air through the widening hole. He downed
tools, headed for the washroom—and met Skeel's cat.

Something was stuck to its fur. O'Malley got near
enough to pluck it out. A stalk with a full head of ripe
wheat attached. The cat sat there contentedly washing itself
while O'Malley thoughtfully picked the wheat to pieces,
watching the grains drop to the floor—as alien in this place
as a fall of moon dust.

He wandered back and came across Skeel in the passage. Skeel's black-rimmed eyes were squinting—he'd just arrived up the steps. "Have you seen my cat?"

"Yes," said O'Malley. "In the washroom."

"Good. As long as he's around."

O'Malley noticed the wetness on his shirt sleeve. You always looked at Skeel when he emerged from the "catacombs," searching for some clue that would tell you what lay behind that pert, noncommittal reticence. "Your sleeve's wet."

"Is it?" Skeel gave a reasonably convincing impression of having just noticed. "Well, I've had a wash."

"You? When—last week?"

Skeel saw the wheat stalk still in O'Malley's hand. "Where did you come across that? Grass, isn't it?"

"No, wheat, I think. It was stuck to your cat."

"Really? That explains it."

"Explains what?"

There was something else about Skeel; a greenish, organic stain on the seat of his denim trousers—and a longing to communicate. "You'll laugh if I tell you." A darting look to and fro. "You won't tell nobody else? It's my cat. I reckon he lost his memory."

Whatever O'Malley had been expecting, it was not this. He waited. "Ever since he come here—my cat, I mean—know what I've been giving him to drink?"

"Milk, of course."

"You got it! And all the while he followed me about like he was my shadow. Had that dazed look, a bit like us really, and then I done a switch."

"Switch?"

"Yeah. I been giving him water." Skeel dropped his

voice to a whisper. "I know where there's water! I kept him off the milk for a couple of days and you know what happened? Yesterday?"

"No."

"He ran away! First time ever. If that's wheat you took off him . . ."

"Yes?"

"Means he's been back."

"Back where?"

"I dunno. Somewhere. Somewhere outside. I've been trying to follow him, you know? But in the end, you can't really follow a cat."

O'Malley suddenly felt as if he'd been hit between the eyes. Absurd, of course, but . . . "Are you trying to say that the milk is doped? And that's why we don't get our memories back?"

Skeel grinned. For the first time O'Malley noticed that he had two teeth missing in the front. "I never exactly *said* that!"

O'Malley followed with an obvious question. "Why didn't you try the experiment on yourself?"

The little eyes looked away. "Never thought of it." The lie was like a cracked bell.

"Where's this water you've found?"

Skeel evidently regretted having given away his secret. "There isn't much left. It started drying up when the rain stopped. It's like a little underground spring. . . ." Skeel knew he couldn't go back on it now. "You'll have to keep your head down. Have you got a flashlight? Mine's pretty near run out again. Bainbridge wouldn't give me a new battery."

"Hang on, I'll fetch it."

The nooks and crannies through which Skeel could crawl

were almost beyond O'Malley's bulkier frame. Arch after arch, low pitched recesses; there was the scutter of unknown life, the tomblike pressure O'Malley remembered all too well from his own first exploration.

At last Skeel's dim flashlight beam beckoned from his place of encampment. O'Malley had a brief illusion of an underground cave, a place with a sound of the sea in his ears.

He shone his own flashlight up at the stone roof, crouching beneath it on his knees. There was a wet patch feeding slow, rhythmical drips into a plastic yogurt jar Skeel had placed under it. The jar had nearly filled. There was a second jar—empty—next to it.

Skeel handed over the full jar. "Have a swig. Only fair to warn you, though—my cat's drunk out of that!"

O'Malley sipped. Brackish but not unpleasant —especially after all those days on goats' milk. He handed the jar to Skeel, but he put it down at once. "Got to go easy on it. Haven't really finished my experiment, yet. Reckon it's all right, trying things out on a cat? Won't hurt him, will it?" There were a lot of things Skeel wasn't saying. His eyes came up from behind his thin flashlight. "Are you going to tell Bainbridge?"

"That's for you to do, isn't it?"

"Yeah—only I want to be sure first—sure about the milk. If I told anybody now, they'd think I was crazy. See?"

"No, not quite!"

Skeel went on, "Anyway, we don't have to tell Bainbridge—not yet. It's not an escape plan."

"Isn't it?" asked O'Malley.

Then he got it! The crafty little devil; he wanted O'Malley to play cat—or guinea pig—because he was too scared to try it himself. That's why he'd shown him the spring.

Skeel said, "Well, you know where it is, now. If you ever fancy it, help yourself. Only leave enough for my cat."

The hole belonged to Landers. He had created it, as he had created fire. And in so far as you could ever read an expression on Landers' face, he deeply resented Bainbridge's rotation system for the excavation.

Never more so than when it happened to be Wheeler's shift—with Hackett bumbling about on his knees, clawing at the stone like an overlarge, ungainly puppy in a garden patch.

"I say, Hackett. Watch what you're doing!" said Landers. "If the whole lot caves in, we'll have to start all over from scratch."

"Scratch is right," grinned Hackett, chipping cheerfully with the mattock blade.

Wheeler hung about, holding the flashlight. His black beard was growing into a point, his eyes like eggs about to hatch into snakes. Landers almost quaked in his presence, and Wheeler knew it, reveled in it.

It was early twilight when O'Malley appeared in the passage. He gave Landers a message. "Special meeting of the Committee—Millie's room."

"Why Millie's?" Landers was petulant, unwilling to leave Hackett and Wheeler in charge. "We're nearly through the wall. Oh, well. Knock off, you chaps. End of shift."

When O'Malley and Landers had gone, Hackett climbed out of the hole. Wheeler asked, "Where you off to, mate?"

"You heard what the man said."

"Who, that nut? He can shove it. Here, *you* hold the flashlight." Wheeler scrambled down, suddenly active. "Where's that bleeding pickaxe?"

"But look, hold on . . ." said Hackett.

"Might as well try and steal a march on them," said Wheeler. "Been waiting for the chance."

He worked in a frenzy. Sparks flew, bits of mortar and stones spat like bullets. Then—no Wheeler!

Hackett knelt down, shone his flashlight into the jet black space—but it was as if the darkness would not receive it. "Where are you, Wheeler?"

Wheeler, somewhere, was laughing. "Come down, Hackett, and bring that lump of hammer."

Hackett hesitated, then went through feet first. The second hole Wheeler had made was a tight fit, but he squeezed through, barking knees and elbows on rough corners.

Hackett lay on his back, swinging the flashlight beam about, trying to get his bearings. Then he saw Wheeler on his knees. In front of him was something that looked like a long but not quite rectangular box.

"Got that hammer? Shine your light. Not at me, you big nit, down on the lid. That's it. . . ." Wheeler hacked and pried, using the tongues of the hammerhead as jimmies. Then he gave a gasp of satisfaction, "Grab hold of the other end, Hackett, and give it a good push."

A hinged lid groaned open. Wheeler and Hackett eased themselves slowly up, supporting the lid's weight so that it wouldn't slam down on their fingers. When it had reached the end of its swing, Wheeler snapped on his flashlight and shone it straight in.

Hackett choked. Wheeler giggled.

In its stone coffin lay a perfect skeleton from which all flesh had long since perished. The last sleep had still preserved for it a lingering humanity; skull, eye sockets, a grimace of mouth with several surviving teeth; horny hands crossed over the upper rib case.

Hackett was shaking now. Wheeler guffawed. "You're thick, Hackett. What do you think he's going to do—jump up and bite you?"

13

TWIN FLASHLIGHTS STOOD ON THE FLOOR OF MILLER'S cell, throwing their reflected light back from the domed ceiling: a different hideousness sat slanted in its wheel-chair, watching with an oblique concern as Bainbridge examined Miller's ankle. "What do you think, O'Malley?"

O'Malley fingered the swelling, as gently as he could, but Miller sobbed with pain. "I don't think it's broken."

Bainbridge said, "Do try and stop that row, old chap. O'Malley says it isn't broken, and who are you to argue with St. John's ambulance brigade?"

"Oh, what's happened *now*?" enquired Landers.

"Miller succeeded in opening a secret door up in what you tell us are the east cloisters. Unfortunately, it was dark at the time and I suppose Millie made the mistake of thinking the door led straight to Euston station. Fortunately, he had enough sense to do a little reconnaissance before committing Conway to a death plunge in his buggy."

Landers frowned. "But look here, if Miller's ankle is broken he's going to need hospitalization."

"Good heavens! You might as well say he needs a fortnight's convalescence in Bournemouth." Bainbridge's voice had a harder edge than usual.

"You're missing the point," went on Landers. "I meant,

the goons, as you call them, will *have* to be contacted, now."

Raxby's beard parted. "You reckon they don't already know?"

"An interesting hypothesis, old boy," said Bainbridge. "And if you don't know what a hypothesis is, Millie, it's what happens to little boys who disregard the Escape Committee and try to be very clever, all by themselves."

"We'll try a cold compress," said O'Malley. "A torn up undershirt will do."

Bainbridge nodded. "Be a good chap, Raxby, and fetch one from the stores. Soak it well on the way back."

"Okay." Raxby glanced at Conway. "Somebody's going to have to look after him."

"Any volunteers?" asked Bainbridge.

O'Malley shrugged. "I'll have a go."

When Raxby returned with the dripping undershirt, his hands were shaking. He stood there, breathing fast, licking his lips, while O'Malley prepared his compress. Then he caught Bainbridge's eye in the flashlight's beam and jerked his head toward the door. Bainbridge followed him out.

"What's up?"

Raxby stopped outside Travers' cell. "You're not going to like this, mate. Hold tight to yourself."

Raxby thrust open the door and shone his flashlight. Bainbridge nearly screamed. "Mother of God!"

The skeleton grinned back at them from the bed, looking so grotesquely alive that it might almost have waved a greeting.

Bainbridge recovered. "Alas, poor Yorick," he quoted. "I knew thee well . . ."

"We can't leave him there," said Raxby.

"I don't see why not. He looks perfectly comfortable to me."

"But the bloke's . . . *dead.*"

"Remarkably observant of you, old boy! Who was last on the tunnel shift?"

"You need to ask?"

"Wheeler, the sod! Yes, it's his style."

"We've got to do *something.*"

"What do you suggest, old chap? I, for one, am not carting that back to the vaults. Let's call him Travers. He'll remind all of us of our own mortality and that sort of thing—what?"

Deep in the night Miller cried softly into his pillow.

He was not fully awake, yet his pain and misery were like icy hands all over him. He turned his face this way and that, as if dodging blows. He dreamed that he was limping on crutches trying to escape from something—something on wheels. Door after door flung itself open in front of him, then he was tumbling down an endless flight of stairs with the crutches clattering after like brooms to beat him.

Was he really awake now or still dreaming? The door of his cell opened and a figure stood there, shadowed in the soft, radiant glow of a lantern. Miller could hear it breathe, a little wheezily. A short, dumpy person entered. He had a bald pate ringed by gray hair and wore a cloak with a hood flung back on his shoulders and a rope cord looped about his waist.

Miller felt the coolness of a hand on his hot brow. The lantern swung gently away. Then his sleeping bag was being unzipped, the crude bandages unwound. Soft fingers caressed Miller's ankle, but he felt no pain. There was the tangy smell of liniment, the cool touch of a new dressing. Then, the rasp of his zipper.

The nostrils whistled, the lantern light hovered briefly close. Through half-closed lids Miller saw a face; large brown eyes, a smiling mouth, a pair of bushy eyebrows . . . then it was dark and the cell door clicked shut.

O'Malley wakened early. Window-bright, strange patterns on his ceiling. He lay watching them for some time, waiting for the lassitude to leave him.

Headache still there. And the humming, like a tiny dynamo fitted to the base of his skull. Something else, though—something different. Not quite a memory—not yet—but a room toward which his forgotten personality wandered, trying to make a homecoming. But it was an inhospitable house, having a glass door locked against his entry. Beyond it, he had a fleeting glimpse of hazy things, half-familiar shapes moving as in smoke.

O'Malley got out of bed and put on his clothes, fighting off another bout of dizziness. He retrieved the plastic jar from his locker, drank a little from it, then put the lid back, squeezed the container into his pocket, opened the door and made his way to Conway's cell.

He'd put Conny to bed himself the previous night. The crippled boy lay there as still as a broken tailor's dummy, his eyes only rolling in consciousness when O'Malley lifted him out and put him in the chair.

O'Malley wondered, again, how Miller managed it: carting Conway around, heaving him up the steep staircase into the quad.

O'Malley hadn't bothered to undress him, though Miller managed even that. There was saliva on his mouth, which

O'Malley wiped away with a tissue. The misshapen hands felt at once for the wheels. O'Malley removed them and folded them on to his lap.

He squeaked the chair along the passage to the delivery shaft. Yes, the day's rations had arrived. He fed Conway. Bits of cold bacon, a small chunk of buttered bread. Conway nibbled it all down, broken teeth grinding, spilling fragments down his chest, which O'Malley picked up and fed back.

Then the water, straight from Skeel's plastic jar. He got as much past Conway's bloated tongue as he could. Poor Conny! It probably wouldn't prove anything, but why should he—O'Malley—be the only guinea pig? No milk for Conway, then. O'Malley was in charge—for now. If Conway regained some sort of memory, how would it show?

O'Malley just wanted to find out, that was all. Like Skeel and his cat. He wouldn't let Conway suffer—if to remember *was* to suffer. He could easily reverse the experiment, couldn't he?

But O'Malley despised himself, suddenly had another dizzy spell, then a short bout of the old craziness. He wanted to lunge a foot at the latest milk churn and send the filthy brew streaming across the floor.

He wheeled Conway to the washroom, lugged him into a stall and restrained an urge to vomit as he exposed the half-nakedness to the pan. How the hell did Miller do this, day after day?

Luckily his bowels weren't working yet. O'Malley yanked the denims into place and got him back into his wheelchair. Conny's eyes rolled—in search of Millie?

On the way back to Millie's cell, O'Malley took a chance, parked the wheelchair, and dived down the steps. At the "spring," Skeel's spare jar was still collecting drips. It was three-quarters full. No cat! O'Malley exchanged the jars and scrambled back. No one about.

Miller was awake.

"How are you feeling?"

Miller was apparently trying to work something out. "Okay."

"Leg hurt?"

"Not much."

"You'll need a new compress."

Miller didn't seem to be listening. "O'Malley, do you dream much?"

"All the time—in technicolor."

"You can't always tell the difference, can you?"

"Between what and what?"

"Dreams . . . and real happenings. I dreamt somebody came in last night, dressed up as a monk. He did something to my ankle."

O'Malley sniffed. That smell . . . he unzipped Miller, took a look, and said, "It wasn't a dream."

Miller squinted down at the new, neat dressing and laughed. "No wonder I feel like I'm floating on air! Reckon I'll be able to walk soon?"

"No hurry."

Miller looked at Conway. "It's him, see? Has he been to the toilet yet?"

"Yes," said O'Malley. "He's had breakfast, too. I'll fetch you some in a minute."

"Thanks. Decent of you to take over, like. I think he fancies you. Look at the way he's watching your face! You get to know his different expressions. He looks daggers at Wheeler! Will you leave him with me for a while? You won't believe it, but sometimes we have a sort of talk."

O'Malley avoided looking too directly at the skeleton propped up in Travers' bed. Bainbridge, Raxby and Landers were there. While O'Malley had been with Miller, they had unloaded the platform and distributed breakfast to the others as they'd arrived. Now they were munching bread and bacon and passing the milk churn round.

"Hello, O'Malley" said Bainbridge. "We were beginning to think you'd escaped! I say, you look a bit pale this morning. Feel all right?"

Vertigo, then suddenly, in perfect duplicate, there were *two* Bainbridges, *two* Raxbys, *two* pale, haunted Landers— two grinning "Travers"!

O'Malley closed his eyes. "Just a headache." He made himself tell them the story of Miller's monk. Raxby glowered at nobody in particular—Bainbridge cut in quickly. "That accounts for the roll of adhesive tape we've found on Travers' bed. I say! If it was that little goon, it's a wonder he didn't drop dead with shock—what? Or perhaps young Miller entertained an angel unawares. The row he was kicking up, he wouldn't need to say a prayer. The Almighty would have picked up the sound waves from the other side of the Milky Way."

Landers' mind was on something else. "O'Malley, have you seen those yogurt jars?"

Bainbridge explained. "Somebody's pinched them. Landers was hoping to use one to make an hour glass. I don't know where he thought he was going to get the sand."

Landers practically whined. "There are too many people helping themselves to things around here. The hammer head's missing, too."

Raxby shrugged. "Who cares? For all the good them tools are, we might as well start a bleeding museum. You and your tunnel, Landers! Look where it got us!" He gave the skeleton a sour look.

Bainbridge said, "We can still press on through the vaults. Landers has admitted to a slight error of geography—not his fault. His navigational aids were struck by lightning, you know. Any day now, he'll be able to tell us exactly where we are—and every little bit helps. For instance, if we learned that once through the outside wall we could hitch a short ride to, say, Manchester Central Station . . ."

"Hertfordshire," said O'Malley.

Bainbridge's eyes were like camera flashes. "What's that, old boy?"

"Ten miles north of Redbridge . . ."

The silence in the cell was like a plate spinning on the floor between them. Only O'Malley could snatch it up before it lost its momentum and rattled irretrievably out of reach.

He blinked at the baffled wall of multiple faces, forced a smile, and said, "It was supposed to be a joke. What are you all staring at me for? It was only a joke . . ."

14

"MY SON, I DON'T QUITE UNDERSTAND WHAT'S GOING ON."

"Neither do I, Father."

"He definitely said, 'ten miles north of Redbridge'?"

"Yes."

"Actually, we are twenty two, as the crow flies. And northeast, rather than north."

"I know. All the same . . ."

"My point is that O'Malley's prescience may have been entirely spontaneous, something arising out of his subconscious. Otherwise he would, surely, have got the details right. As you know, before they underwent treatment the lads were told precisely where they would subsequently be sent. It was thought to be a useful, if secondary, test of the drug's effectiveness. No one else, not even Landers, has ever ventured even a rough approximation?"

"No."

"Of course, O'Malley was always considered a special case. The clinical tests, however, were fairly conclusive."

"*Fairly,* Father?"

A short pause on the hot line. "My son, had there been *no* doubt, there would scarcely be an experimental factor at all, would there? You attended the course of lectures at Golders·Green? Amnesia is normally the result of a traumatic experience in the patient's life—a blow on the head, an emotional shock—and in appropriate cases the victim may make what is called a psychoneurotic escape from memories which he cannot endure. While the condition persists—the fugue state as it is called—he may live a perfectly logical and orderly life, though frequently with considerable personality change and, perhaps, minor deficiencies such as a degree of confusion about time and place. A further curious feature of amnesia, as a natural phenomenon, a mere sickness, is that when he recovers from it the patient forgets everything that has happened to him during the fugue state. You follow?"

Bainbridge thought of Golders Green. "He has no recollection of what's happened between losing his memory and finding it again. So he's left to pick up the threads from where he left off."

"Exactly. Which is one reason why Compound Y may be regarded as something of a 'wonder drug.' Quite different in its effects. No recovery of memory, so no fugue state, no threads to pick up, as you put it. To all intents and purposes their past lives ceased to be from the moment they awoke in their new environment. So we, my son, have a unique opportunity of setting their feet on new paths. No outside intervention, no troublesome relatives, for instance, to make demands or plague the boys with anxieties as to their origin. You have fully grasped the implications, the measure of our responsibility?"

"I think so, Father."

A more evangelical tone entered into the Abbot's voice: "It is our privilege to offer them all a fresh start, a new Garden of Eden! What was it, my son, that brought them to the brink of damnation? On the one hand, being twisted and broken by human brutality. On the other, falling into such depravity that Society thought them irredeemable. They suffered inhumanity? Therefore we must be humane and our continued endeavors will heal them, we pray, for ever. They were ensnared by vice? So, as far as possible, we shall remove temptation. They hated and despised Authority? But, during this phase of their treatment, there will be no visible authority for them to tilt at. They were once self-indulgent? Ah, so we shall deprive them of all but bare sustenance! They are forming new identities on which to build new values, entirely new lives."

"Yes, Father."

A drop of tone. "So you can understand that your reports are disquieting. This lack of will to survive, the despondency you mention. Miller's accident—he really should have been better supervised, you know! And O'Malley's curious piece of recall. Are you quite sure, my son, that you have administered the supplementary drugs correctly? They're *most* critical. The overall effect should have been to render the subjects quiescent as regards interpersonal relationships, while, at the same time, preserving their determination to come face to face with newly discovered realities. It would rather defeat our objective, would it not, if we had to come down there and drag them out screaming? We want 'escapes,' my son, not all this aimless fidgeting! By the way, the antidote . . ."

"Yes, Father?"

"It is still in your safe keeping?"

"Of course!"

"This O'Malley business . . . it's just occurred to me that one of the lads *could* have got hold of a syringe. Hackett, you say, spends a lot of time in the chapel."

"But he couldn't possibly get in here! It wouldn't even occur to him to try."

"All the same, I'd be obliged if you'd check. After all the counterdrug is the *only* method of deliberately reversing the permanent effects of Compound Y. At least we can be sure of that."

Bainbridge opened the shallow desk drawer, saw the emergency candles and matches, a few bits of junk, the pens and pads he used for his hurried but more detailed reports—and at the back, two primed hypodermics. The containers were labeled ANTIDOTE—clear, black, and large, like the caption in a comic cartoon film.

He pushed the drawer shut, loud enough for the Abbot to hear on his telephone. "All present and correct, Father."

"Well, take good care of them, my son. Personally, I was against the provision of a counterdrug, but one doesn't argue with the Home Office, which evidently foresaw some possible misadventure that, frankly, eludes me! By the way, they have authorized the tear gas. It'll be delivered today. An extreme measure, of course. On the whole, I think it would be more expedient for you to arrange Wheeler's 'escape' as soon as possible. His next tunnel shift . . . Brother Francis is already removing some bricks in the vault foundation. It will be interesting to see whether Hackett follows the young rascal! In any case, we shall be standing by to pick them up. Contrive, somehow, that Landers and the others don't all swarm through at the same time—we can't cope with a crowd. Besides, the Home Office want us to try out Phase Four, first."

"Phase Four?"

"You can't have forgotten! Purely experimental. The effect of Compound Y, together with the accumulation of other medication, upon the undernourished human organism and the emancipated personality. Don't worry, my son, you won't have to participate directly, I assure you! I'll let you know as soon as I receive confirmation—I'm getting in touch with the Home Office this morning. Excellent rapport. Rather gratifying in these days when there is so little real cooperation elsewhere between Church and State. It helped, of course, in the beginning, that our Order was able, for obvious reasons, to undertake the project without too great a burden on the Treasury in these difficult times. . . . Are you still there, my son?"

"Yes, Father."

Pause. "Something tells me that you have lost a little of your old zeal! No wonder, my son, no wonder. It would be a pity at this critical stage, but we could pull you out, if you wished. We've received an application from a young man—a Community Service Volunteer. Excellent credentials. Winchester. Played Rugby for his school. Going up to Cambridge in the autumn—he could see us through the next stage. You could devise your own escape; then it would be easy enough for us to slip the new chap in— under the name of Travers, of course. As you know, this is an exigency we have always borne in mind. Well, let us know—today, if possible. Oh, and talking of Travers . . . you'd better do something about the skeleton that young imp Wheeler disinterred. Poor Brother Ambrose got quite a nasty shock—not that it was less than he deserved!"

When he'd replaced the phone, Bainbridge looked for a long time at the barely perceptible cracks in the opposite wall. Like the outline of the door to a storage cupboard—in which an officiating priest had once kept the Means of Grace. In fact, it led through a labyrinthine passage up old steps and straight to the monk's quarters.

A way to a makeshift, pre-Copernican Heaven, thought

Bainbridge? He had been brought up in the faith and, away from this mounting madness, regularly gave his lips to the cup and accepted the wafer on his tongue.

But Father Ignatius, he decided disloyally—who should presume to judge him?—was a complacent little Jehovah ruling a tin, shaky cosmos. He'd created it—and found it Good. His bizarre and shoddy Garden of Eden, inhabited by a handful of unlikely Adams not yet knowing how naked they were!

Had O'Malley, somehow, hit upon the Tree of Knowledge? Some Eve! As for the serpent . . . Wheeler wasn't escaping through that vault. Not yet . . . or not at all. That would be too easy—for Wheeler, for Bainbridge. Bainbridge hadn't been to Winchester and he'd never played Rugby. But Wheeler was his "client"—and the hell if he'd turn him loose; not just like that. What sort of social worker pushed his client through a hole in a wall—for somebody else to be spat at?

If everything went wrong, would Father Ignatius become an angry deity? Send down fire and pestilence? Or, perhaps, be content with a small plague of locusts?

Come off it, Bainbridge, old boy, he thought. You're getting the Good Book out of sequence.

Skeel was like one of those more docile animals captured from the wild, accepting its cage without fret, with no painful nostalgia, no yearning for lost freedom; only an immediate preoccupation with pressing its nose against unfamiliar bars, sniffing out a bowl of corn, marking the boundaries of its confines, investigating the novel possibilities of an exercise wheel.

So, when some time ago, deep in the mysterious belly of

the "catacombs," he'd hit upon the hole, he'd kept it to himself.

It was late evening, with the sun sinking out of view, but Skeel had lost the sun.

He'd brought the hammerhead he'd pinched, and now, having worked a few things out, he began hacking away at the narrow cavity of heavy stones. With almost alarming ease he loosened the mortar and a huge chunk of rock fell away—so fast that if he hadn't dodged out of the way it might have crushed his chest. Skeel was lying on his back at the time, dim flashlight in his mouth, mining his way through the rock.

When the dust had settled and he'd finished choking, he began to feel with his outstretched hand into the cavity opening above him. There was a moment of excitement when the first puff of wind brushed his face and tousled his hair, making him gasp with wonder and adventure.

He climbed, inch by inch, and presently he found himself without further impediment on a short, steep slope of dusty stonework smelling of all the ages. Still the silence was tomblike. He said to himself, "Christ!"—a little prayer, perhaps, to the Unknown. For this newly born Skeel, miracles just happened.

He used his fingernails to test places, probing for the best grip and he was never once denied. He made a slow ascent. The draft of air seemed to come alive, whistling on a low note, calling him on. He hacked with his hammerhead, sometimes using it like a mattock to chip with, sometimes like a climber's hook to bite itself into a crevice—and up and up he went.

Little stones and chippings rattled behind him. The cavity became smaller so that he had to squeeze through it, bracing his small, strong shoulders. Then, suddenly, it was bigger, much bigger. The draft of air positively howled in his ears.

Skeel spat out bits of dust and stone. More stones wiggled to and fro, then loosened and fell. It was now quite a long time before they hit the bottom.

Even Skeel was surprised when his hands discovered what was unmistakably a stone stair. He took his light out of his mouth and directed the faint beam upwards. Crikey—stairs! Going round and round in a spiral, soon vanishing from view but, according to some sensible logic, obviously going on and on—right up to the top somewhere.

The air became swifter still and sweeter; a sort of sigh, thought Skeel. Up he went—then he saw stars! *Real* stars in a black dome of sky.

And something else—something between Skeel and that circle of sky. At first Skeel could make nothing of it. He climbed on and on, soft shoes rustling on the dusty steps; then he saw a shape that resembled a large, cloaked figure . . . waiting at the top.

Like a sort of giant monk!

Skeel approached him with discretion, and when he was right at the very top, he stretched up a hand to touch.

Hard—and cold! Not human after all. He pushed, and there came, out of the night, a deep, metallic note uttered as if in protest.

A bell! It went on swinging, emitting tiny, muffled tolls before coming to a rest.

Two more steps and Skeel found himself on a firm surface with air breathing at him from all directions. He was leaning on a wooden ledge, just the right height, arms akimbo. Surrounded by an immense starlit sky, he was looking down on the silver-edged darkness of open countryside. Yes . . . he could make out the shapes of buildings and, much farther away, the twinkling constellations of what was perhaps a town or large village.

Nearer, a dog barked at the night—perhaps barked at Skeel. Away from the eclipsing bell, the moon swung free and bright. Gradually, more shapes emerged; a house! Not far away, either. Lights shining upstairs and downstairs.

Then new light spilled out of the house. It came from a room behind the door. The door had just been opened. Quite clearly, Skeel saw the girl.

A girl swinging a pail, making her way down the path lit by the light from the door. Skeel leaned over the belfry edge and tried flashing his light, on and off—and feeble though it was, the girl must have spotted it.

She stopped, halfway along the garden path. She looked up. Skeel could see her face quite clearly in the moonlight; a small, round, moon-face.

There was a big shed near the house. Something mooed inside. A cow! At the door the girl stopped, put down her bucket, and lifted her face.

Skeel called out, "Hi!"

"Hi!" said the girl.

That was all—this time. The girl went into the shed and closed the door behind. Inside, the cow mooed again. The moon shone down. The night whispered.

That rotten Bainbridge! Skeel's flashlight just didn't have enough strength left to shine far down the wall.

Not that it had even occurred to him to try and climb down. He only wanted to shout at the girl again, but she was too long with the cows.

15

NO ONE KNEW WHAT WHEELER HAD DONE TO CONWAY—IF anything. All Bainbridge and Raxby could be sure of was that something like a pitched battle had raged in the Common Room and they had arrived at the tail end of it.

Conway was in the middle, furniture scattered around him, shrieking and whirling himself like a top, crooked knuckles clenched white on his wheel rims.

Hackett was perched on top of the bookcase, presumably trying to keep his legs clear. A sliver of wood a foot long dangled from the shattered desk by a thread, and books had been wrenched from their shelves and lay torn and twisted across the floor.

Wheeler had got himself jammed in a corner with the broken desk as a barricade. He was smirking, but there was an expression in his eyes akin to surprise and horror, especially when Conway swivelled yet again, shrieked, gibbered, and tried to batter the desk to pieces.

"For chrissake, get him out!" said Wheeler. "He's gone completely nuts."

"What brought it on—you?" asked Raxby.

"I never done nothing! Not a thing. Right, Hackett? We was just in here, playing craps—and the door bust open and he went straight for us. Look at the mess he's made."

Conway abandoned his assault on the desk and slewed his chair at Bainbridge. His face was contorted, eyes staring crookedly, saliva squirting from the awful mouth. Bainbridge dodged aside, grabbed the push handle and held on.

"Where the hell is O'Malley?"

Raxby said, "With Millie, I think."

"Hackett, you clown, come off your perch and run and fetch him!"

Hackett climbed down, face petrified, and picked himself a circuitous route out of reach—he thought—of Conway's wheels. But Conway, wrenching free of Bainbridge's hold, got Hackett in the doorway, screaming and launching himself at Hackett's shins.

Hackett winced, limped through the door and Conway was after him—a terrible human missile hurling itself along the cloisters. Hackett made it to the steps. Conway hesitated at the top; if he'd had an ounce of muscle in his paralyzed legs, he might have flung himself down. As it was the powerful arms braced on the wheels—then, at the last moment, a fresh idea seemed to occur to whatever brain he had. He turned about, suddenly deadly quiet, the wayward gaze trying to fix itself on Raxby and Bainbridge twenty strides away. "Hold tight!" said Raxby. "The poor bleeder's going to charge us."

"I know, old boy. When he arrives, let's try getting a hold on one wheel each; then we'll cart him down to Miller."

Raxby chewed, calm and thoughtful. "He's been moody since Millie fell down that hole, but this . . . what's happened to him?"

Conway charged. Bainbridge said, "Save your breath, old chap, and watch your fingers in the spokes."

The chair clattered along the cloister with the acceleration of a small car. At the last moment Raxby planted a strategic toe on the chair step and, as Conway spun, Bainbridge jammed him against the wall. The shock of the impact calmed Conway—long enough, at least, for them to get him back to the steps and carry him down.

Miller was sitting on the edge of his bed, gingerly trying out his injured ankle with short, still painful jabs on the straw mat. O'Malley stood in attendance, presumably trying his hand as physiotherapist.

Miller looked at Conway with that strangely unfathomable devotion. "What have you been doing to him?"

"It's what he tried to do to us, mate," said Raxby.

O'Malley said, "I thought he'd be all right on his own for a while. It's sunny in the quad."

Miller winced and took his foot off the floor. "He misses me, I suppose. Has he been to the toilet and all that? He looks hot. There's some milk left in my cup—O'Malley put it on the locker."

"I'll fetch it," said Bainbridge.

Raxby had a fleeting thought: Bainbridge running his own errands?

Bainbridge fed the milk to Conway, gently squeezing his nose, ignoring the dribbles, the toss to and fro of the odd-shaped head.

O'Malley watched expressionlessly. A muscle twitched in his cheek. Once he met Bainbridge's eye—then looked away.

Raxby was kneeling beside Conway's chair—chipping, banging with his bare hands. As each wheel hub sprang off and clattered away, he worried out the split pins with thumb and finger. He worked on all of them—big wheels, small wheels—before supporting the chair against his shoulder, pulling off the wheels and letting them roll to the wall.

The chair, and Conway, sat square and immobile—and Miller didn't like it. "Why didn't you chop his legs off and be done with it?"

Raxby grinned, without malice. "Better this way, Millie—better for you, for us, for him. Until he quiets down."

"He's quiet now!"

"He's had a tiring day," said Raxby.

Bainbridge said, "I expect he was just thirsty."

"Or," said O'Malley, "there's something he's forgotten!"

"Forgotten?" said Miller.

"Forget it!" said O'Malley. Double talk—he shouldn't have blurted it out. He'd have to watch his tongue.

He knew that both Raxby and Bainbridge were watching him, waiting . . . for what? But O'Malley had the sudden illusion that he could see into Conway's soul. What was the torment in those crooked eyes? A terrible darkness—or an even more terrible light?

Conway rocked, to and fro, to and fro, a young child's drool frothing on his lips.

Later, Bainbridge came into O'Malley's cell. He stood by the door for a moment, waiting for O'Malley to turn his head. Then he heeled the door closed, smiled his old smile, came across to the bed, hands in pockets, and sat at O'Malley's foot. "Thought we might have a chat, old boy."

"Go ahead."

"That Freudian slip of yours . . . Hertfordshire."

"Oh, that!"

"Yes, that. Something tells me it wasn't just a wild guess. Ten miles north of Redbridge, eh?"

O'Malley sat up, stark-faced, fingering his beard. "Or maybe a hundred miles south of Venezuela."

"No, you can't get out of it as easily as that. You spoke with the ringing tones of an oracle. How was it done?"

O'Malley gave him a faint grin. He saw no point, now, in prolonging what had become a farce. "The milk . . . I think that's what they put the dope in. I've been dodging it."

"What with—carbolic and water?"

"Skeel found a spring. . ."

"A *what?*"

"Well, a sort of leak, down in the foundations. Rain water, probably—it's practically dried up now. Skeel collected it and tried it out on his cat!"

Bainbridge laughed. O'Malley was too self-absorbed to notice the dumbfounded expression cross his face. "Is that what happened to the yogurt jars? I rather hope, old boy, the stuff came straight from the skies and not via some filthy drain. Did Skeel persuade you to try it out first? Apart from the cat, I mean."

"Not exactly."

"Then what, exactly?"

Another weary shrug from O'Malley. "It just occurred to me . . . well, it seemed possible. We couldn't drink the water supply so it had to be the milk, didn't it?"

"And now you have proof that the amnesia drug, or whatever it is, comes ready mixed in the milk churns? How long have you managed to stay off it?"

"A couple of days—I think. Not much more. And I wouldn't call it proof."

"But you've started getting your memory back?"

"I don't know. Well, yes—in bits. Unless they're just bits of nightmares! Tell you what, though, they've laced the bloody milk with *something*. Man, the withdrawal symptoms . . . by now I've seen everything, including snakes crawling up the wall!"

Bainbridge's eyebrows shot up. "Good heavens . . . I do believe you tried out this little ploy on poor Connie!"

"I'm not proud of that."

"What else?"

"What else what?"

"Your memory, old boy. Or have you forgotten?"

"No . . . but I'd rather wait, if you don't mind. I want to be . . . sure."

The tear gas equipment had arrived on Bainbridge's desk. Nozzle, cylinder with shoulder straps, flexible hose connection frayed in several places—the damn thing probably leaked.

There was also a little picnic box packed tight with edibles; fruit, two hard boiled eggs, a couple of the crusty homebaked loaves; butter, cheese . . . No milk. Instead, three tins of coke.

So you're one of Society's privileged now, old boy! He pushed everything aside and lifted the phone.

"But it's all quite impossible, my son!"

"Yes, Father."

"This seepage . . . I thought we'd agreed to curtail young Skeel's perambulations?"

"I tried."

"Not with much success, apparently! I must consult Brother Bruce about the drains . . . I don't wish to alarm you, but I can't help wondering. Do you happen to know the symptoms of typhoid fever?"

"They'll all have had their inoculations, won't they?"

"I must check that with the Home Office . . . but they can't have been inoculated against every known disease."

"Oh, well, we must hope for the best," Father Ignatius went on. "Most unfortunate that they succeeded in pulling the wool over your eyes. But two or three days off their tranquilizers would account for the behavior of O'Malley and Conway. By the way, the sooner you can get Miller back on his feet the better. He's probably malingering— Brother Ambrose says he suffering only a slight sprain."

"But the breakdown of their amnesia, Father . . ."

"Hardly the milk—or their abstinence from it!"

"That's not what O'Malley thinks. Anyway, the drug— there *must* have been some miscalculation."

"Not conclusive, my son. Not at all conclusive. Certainly not in poor Conway's case. To have any idea what he remembered, or otherwise, we should have to use clairvoyance, would we not? As for O'Malley, who is already contaminated by heroin and goodness knows what . . he rather confuses the issue."

"Yes, but. . ."

"Well, then. Even science hasn't *all* the answers! I can hardly go to the Home Office and inform them, purely on the basis of your vague suspicions, that their wonder drug is not infallible. What will they think of us—of our Order? Now are you ready for Phase Four? And about Wheeler's escape . . . Brother Francis has met with some temporary difficulty. However, he seems to think he can penetrate the vault wall within a day or two. Meanwhile, in case the lads react rather badly to their all-milk diet, triple their doses. You understand?"

During the night O'Malley opened his eyes, sharp awake, with moonlight on the ceiling. He was sure there was a second bed beside him.

Not that it mattered; the discovery merely brought a moment's irritation because he'd got used to being alone, didn't really want a cell mate. He thought, perhaps, that Travers had arrived at last and Bainbridge had dragged his bed in here so that it wouldn't be in the way of the stores.

Yes . . . O'Malley half sat up and looked across. On the edge of the second bed someone was watching him. Unkempt brown beard, dulled eyes, a face that was, perhaps, habitually serious and thoughtful. But now, in the bright moonlight, the man's lips held a touch of mockery. "Mulligan."

"Mulligan? Hi—my name's O'Malley."

The stranger laughed.

"What's funny?"

"Sure, you must have been dreaming," said the stranger. "Your name's not O'Malley!"

"What the hell do you mean? 'My godfathers and god-mothers in my baptism. . .' "

"But you've got it all wrong, man. You must have forgotten."

"Forgotten?"

"The street. Think of a street. Have you got it?"

O'Malley thought, soberly, then nodded. "Yes. I don't remember the town. . ."

"Liverpool."

"What about the street?"

"It has houses and shops. Most streets have, haven't they? And there was a druggist. Harmless old boy. Amos, they called him."

"What about him?"

"Him? It's you we're talking about, O'Malley. There you were, bright boy at college, lining up a nice career for yourself. Art student, weren't you? What by all the saints, brought you to knife that poor old bastard?"

"Knife?"

"Don't echo me, O'Malley! Just tell the truth. Know yourself—it'll be better in the end. You knifed him. Look at the blood on your hands."

O'Malley spread his hands in front of his face. "I couldn't help it."

"Oh, come off it, O'Malley! I know what happened—I was there. Supposed to be a late night druggist, wasn't he? Only not late enough for you. He wouldn't sell you the stuff—old Amos, I mean. And man, you were desperate. You went for him with a knife. Maybe you only meant to scare hell out of him, but he smashed an empty bottle and came for you. Who would have thought the old boy had it in him? Your plea of self-defense . . . didn't cut much ice in court did it, O'Malley? You were lucky to be chosen for the Project, lucky your priest spoke up for you and could pull a few strings. Good thing you had friends. What about the enemy, O'Malley?"

"The enemy?"

"You, man—you! *You* are your enemy. And *what's* your name?"

"Mulligan!"

"That's better! Now say it again. You won't need the Catechism."

"Mulligan!"

The howl in his head stopped, but he was shaking, shaking. . .

The space beside him was empty. No extra bed, no watching figure—nothing.

His head sank back on the rubber pillow and he sobbed, biting his lower lip till it bled.

16

NEXT DAY. THERE WAS NO PANIC YET, BUT LITTLE GROUPS hung about at the shaft staring hopefully up at the bright green glass.

A milk churn had arrived, presumably at the crack of dawn. Bigger than usual. Raxby rolled it on its rim to Travers' cell and draped a sleeping bag over it to cool it from the sun, and Bainbridge ladled the contents out to all comers.

Hackett, expression that of a cuckoo fledgling, gulped down his ration in a single draught, Adam's apple like a yo-yo; Skeel stayed chirpy and unconcerned. Landers' eyes were hunted, Wheeler's suspicious. Raxby sipped noisily, grimacing, dark gaze over the rim of his cup fastened, for some reason, on Bainbridge. O'Malley took cups along to Miller and Conway.

The rest of the day was less eventful than Bainbridge expected. Sun over the quad, people doing their own thing, keeping apart. No trouble, even from Wheeler—or was he cooking something up? He squatted a lot of the time in the wrecked Common Room, shaking his dice, winning the last of Hackett's chewing gum.

Chewing gum! No fresh supplies of that, either. Evidently "God" hadn't thought it necessary any longer. There were no more nightly deliveries or visits—human or edible —so no need for sleeping potions to discourage hanky-panky in the dorm!

Landers messed about with his gadgets; O'Malley, pale and shaky, made bedside visits to Miller and the restless but firmly rooted Conway.

Bainbridge felt he was walking a tightrope stretched across the day. When he'd called off work on the "tunnel," nobody had argued. "No point in slogging our guts out on empty stomachs. I'll pass the word round as soon as manna drops from Heaven." Bainbridge wanted to know just when Brother Francis hacked through the vault wall. Then *he'd* decide who, if anyone, was to be pushed through the hole.

There was a meeting that evening of the Committee— only they hadn't managed to find Landers. Raxby stared balefully at "Travers'" skeleton. "Reckon they're trying to starve us out?"

"Hardly *out,* old boy," said Bainbridge, watching O'Malley's cheek twitch. "It's probably only a temporary fault. Maybe the wagon they use has blown a gasket. On the other hand, 'God' could be trying out a self-denial week—a desperate attempt to save our souls through tribulation. He probably thinks we're getting soft and overfed. We slipped up there. We should have had everybody out on the quad doing push-ups before breakfast in full view of the heavenly host."

Raxby said, "I've got a hunch they've all gone off! I've been watching that bleeding watch tower. Not a glimmer all day."

"I hope you're wrong, old boy. Makes one feel stranded and unloved, like a baby dumped on a church doorstep. Speaking personally, though, I think we're almost better off without their rotten food. No doubt they'll open the shop again in due course. Meanwhile, watch out for Wheeler. He's been crawling about all day with a cannibalistic gleam in his eyes. And have you noticed that Skeel's cat is missing?

Bainbridge started out on one of his tricky trails to the chapel, uncertain as to why he was going. To get away from O'Malley's shakes and silences? Or Raxby's shifty up-and-down glances?

It wasn't to pick at the food they'd left for him; that, he thought, would be just another act of treachery. Treachery? To this bunch of villains and broken reeds? Did he owe them any sort of loyalty? Yes . . . yes, he did!

What's happened to your objectivity, Bainbridge—all that stuff they hammered into you at college? You cared, but did not become emotionally involved, remember? They were cases, to be approached with benign detachment. You observed, you listened, you advised where you thought appropriate; you sipped half a cup of tepid tea, smiled reassuringly, carefully avoided promises—then went away and wrote a report. Nothing more. Only saints kissed lepers; and no crucifixions, please! So why lay off the food now, Bainbridge? What will that prove? Who will know, or care?

And what was he going to tell Father Ignatius—that Raxby was bristling with suspicion and that if O'Malley didn't get a "fix" soon he'd crack wide open?

Then he knew what he really wanted: the telephone. Just the telephone—because it had become an umbilical cord? Not to a mother but to a Father. Kinky! Hell, if I ever get out of here, he thought, I'm going straight to the Labour Exchange. Then get married and beg for a mortgage and a nice big housing loan to go with it; I'll do all those sane, civilized, ordinary things that the carefree, unemployed young do these days.

Somebody was in the chapel? Not Hackett—or not *only* Hackett. The sounds were too subtle, too furtive. Someone was waiting. Watching him through tiny gaps in one of those piles of rubbish and broken pews.

Outside, a dying sun bled on the bits of stained glass. Bainbridge narrowed his flashlight beam, shrugged away his apprehension. Even if he was right, what point was there in a challenge, a confrontation with madness lurking behind a barricade? Perhaps that damned tear gas would be useful after all. . . .

He felt for his key and turned the sanctum lock . . . and they were on him at once, flashlights blazing in his face. Wheeler and Landers, both with bits of pew in their hands. And Hackett, oafishly standing back as if trying to demonstrate that he was the unwilling victim of a press gang.

The first of Wheeler's blows struck his shoulder, sending him reeling back into the sanctum, door swinging in against the wall. Wheeler's light beam followed. "You can skip the karate, mate. It won't work this time. Where's the bleeding light switch?"

He found it, clicked it down with his elbow. "Nice little place you've got here, *Smithy!*"

Smithy!

Wheeler's eyes dropped to the desk. Telephone, food, cylinder. He pulled open the drawer, rifled through the contents, began filling his pockets. Bainbridge lunged at him, but the bit of pew came up again. He was gashed on the temple this time, spots of blood spattering on the desk.

"I did warn you, Smithy."

It was all Wheeler. Hackett was still dithering outside, while Landers stared wildly on, club hanging limply at his side.

Bainbridge watched the candles and matches vanish into Wheeler's denims. "If I were you, old boy, I should keep that lot out of Landers' reach. If you're thinking of starting a beautiful friendship, watch out. How much of his memory has *he* got back?"

"Enough to be getting on with, mate. I can take care of Landers. I'm taking care of everybody see? You can cut preaching at me—haven't I had a belly full of that from you? Who do you reckon you are—Smithy? Call yourself a social worker? You couldn't referee a bleeding kids' football match!" A third vicious blow—and Bainbridge didn't see it coming this time.

His head exploded in flames.

Groggily he returned to consciousness, blood congealing in his hair. How much later was it? Get up and do something, Bainbridge, he told himself—you're wasting the taxpayers' money.

They hadn't bothered to switch the light off. Everything was gone—food, drink, tear gas, candles, and matches; his watch, even a couple of useless old keys, which somebody had once dropped into the drawer. Some of his rough notes were torn up and scattered. The telephone cord had been wrenched from the wall—good-bye, Father!

The antidote! One of the syringes was missing, the second still at the back of the drawer, lodged behind a couple of spare writing pads. Bainbridge pocketed it, then slumped a long time on his chair, mopping at his wounds, trying to collect his senses.

No sign that they'd noticed or tried to open the secret

door. Where had they gone, then? What did Wheeler think he was going to do? Or Landers? Hunt round, in vain, for a couple of doors that would match those thrown-away keys? Possibly . . . it might be the only time left to buy.

He staggered up at last, switched off the light, eased open the door they'd slammed on him. Yale type—no way of locking him in, luckily.

Chapel dark, no sound, no breath. Nor in the moonlit cloisters. How soon before they got to Miller and Conway; Skeel, O'Malley, and Raxby? Wheeler would be careful about Raxby, of course.

He groped down the stone stairs. Flashlight gone, too, but he managed to fumble his way to Travers' cell. Relieved—or afraid?—when he found them both there.

How much had O'Malley let spill to Raxby by now? How long had he been away? An hour? Half?

They looked up as he came in. The sight of his blood-stained face seemed, paradoxically, to steady O'Malley. He got up, said something about dressing it, began fussing around for adhesive tape. Bainbridge shrugged off his solicitude. Raxby chewed, glared, asked no questions, face perhaps deliberately unsympathetic.

"All I want is to lie down. Sorry, Travers, old son!" He tried to lift the skeleton from the bed and prop it on the floor. It abruptly broke in two. Bainbridge said, "Sorry, old chap."

A waste of wit—nobody laughed.

Then Raxby said, "You bastard, Bainbridge." That was all.

Bainbridge closed his eyes. "We all have our faults. And in case you're interested, the name's Smith."

O'Malley's mouth trembled. He said, shaking his head in

urgent protest, "I didn't tell him much. I don't *know* much. We didn't even know your name was Smith."

"Forget it!" Same tired old joke. "First things first. Wheeler's on the rampage. I gather you don't know that, either? He's got Landers in tow—and Hackett, for what that's worth. They're prowling about somewhere like the three musketeers. They raided my place."

"What place?" Raxby scowled.

"A sort of . . . headquarters, if you like. It's in the chapel. I had a key to that, and one to the cloisters, from the start. That first time you found me, and I said I was trying to pick the lock, I'd just come back—you nearly caught me."

"Back from doing what?"

"Receiving instructions. There is—or was—a telephone of sorts. Look, I'm trying to level with you . . . at any moment the balloon's going to go up. Believe it or not, Raxby, I want to help both of you."

O'Malley said, "We've been trying to work it out. We guessed some of it."

Raxby added, "Especially about you, mate. I half tumbled to you a while back, and if I'd only been sure . . ."

"He was just doing his job, Raxby."

"Yeah, some people make a living cleaning out drains!"

O'Malley went on, "This headquarters, as you call it. There's a way through . . . to *them?*"

"Only in theory, old boy." Smith was still playing Bainbridge. "A crafty little door—I don't think our friend Wheeler noticed. And I've never had a key to that. It was a case of 'don't call us, we'll call you.' I rather think they didn't quite trust me not to chicken out, without handing in my notice in triplicate. All they gave me was, so to speak, a false wig—and a regulation hair shirt. In that respect, I've always been just one of you."

Raxby sneered, "Except, no doubt, you got eggs and chips for dinner!"

O'Malley was solicitous again. "Your head's still bleeding."

"Or was it ketchup?" said Raxby.

"What exactly did Wheeler get hold of?"

"Candles, matches, a couple of old keys. Oh, and a cylinder of tear gas—a little gift from 'God' in case someone should assault my virginity."

"Keys?" asked Raxby.

"No need to get excited, old boy. They're useless, but Wheeler doesn't know that yet—I hope. That's why we've got just a little time to chew the rag—before he gets disappointed and tries to overwhelm us with his three-man riot squad. We'd better not be too long, though . . ."

"So they haven't got Skeel with them?" said Raxby.

"Who on earth ever got Skeel anywhere?"

O'Malley said, "Landers is the lock specialist."

"I rather think the poor chap has other things on his mind just now. His past, mainly."

Raxby wriggled. "Look, Bainbridge or Smith or whoever you are, when are you going to tell us the bleeding score? O'Malley thinks he remembers things—things he won't talk much about—but I don't."

"All right," said Bainbridge, eyes open on Raxby. "But I warn you, you're not going to like it."

O'Malley said, "This is an experimental project, yes? Run by some monks, though probably they're only go-betweens. In a way Raxby was right. This is a jail, and we're all doing time. Only there's a lot more to it than that.

We're being used to try out a new drug—something that is supposed to make us forget our past lives and have the chance of a fresh start. How am I doing so far?"

"Extraordinarily well, old boy."

"And you never went to some potty prep school in Bucks."

"No . . . it was called Clapham High Street Primary, actually."

"Anyway," O'Malley continued, "they planted you down here, masquerading as one of us, presumably because of some theory that open supervision would lead to trouble—violence, that sort of thing. The pattern had to be different from the usual set-up, or was it just that this was cheaper?"

"Not quite that!"

"You were very clever, Bainbridge."

"Thanks."

"We've never met, have we?"

"No."

"There's still a lot I don't remember. Huge blanks."

Raxby had been listening, big head switching between them like a spectator at a tennis match. "Just as I always said. Bleeding screwy! And nobody asked our permission to double as guinea pigs."

"I rather think they did," said O'Malley. "I remember bits of an interview. There was a monk . . . tall, lantern-faced character with a deep voice. Another, much smaller chap next to him, wearing his old school tie. That's all I recall, except . . ."

"They gave you an option?" asked Bainbridge.

"*What* option?" Raxby asked, clenching his fists.

"In your case, old boy, between *this* or yet another interminable spell in one of Her Majesty's inglorious prisons, waiting for the judge to decide how best to get you out of his hair." Bainbridge dropped his half-closed eyes to the bunched knuckles. "I'll put you out of your misery, Raxby. You've never actually killed anybody, so far. But occasionally you will lose your temper and bash people's teeth in outside some pub in the King's Road. Apart from that, and a few post office robberies, you're what they call good material."

"Thanks a lot!" said Raxby. "But you still haven't explained nothing much."

"I'm trying. The funny thing is that, crazy or not, the scheme might almost have worked. It could still, in your case—and perhaps with Skeel, Hackett, even Miller. With your pasts wiped out, your personalities remolded, all they'd have to do next is give you a cover story—a fabricated life history you could accept. Some harmless fairy tale about having been brought up by an uncle in Australia who, before he conveniently died, shipped you back to the mother country to be treated in hospital for brain fever, unfortunately contracted in the Bush. I exaggerate slightly. Anyway, along you'd go, having made your escape from this mysterious cage—that, by the way, is supposed to be a test of your will to survive in a new identity—to be recaptured and put on a conveyor belt and carried along to the next stage of rehabilitation. Training programs, that sort of thing. Raxby would be turned into a hearty village blacksmith, O'Malley a self-respecting bank clerk complete with a wife and apartment. Got it?"

O'Malley said, "You never really went along with all that?"

"Not entirely. Mind you, I'm being less than fair."

"And something's gone wrong? The drug?"

"Yes . . . or probably."

"But it must have been tested."

"Oh, yes. With rats. The trouble is, the rats were normal. Like Raxby, Skeel, Hackett, Miller."

"Why only . . . us?" Raxby was looking now at O'Malley, whose face had turned to chalk.

"Sorry, O'Malley . . ." said Bainbridge.

"Mulligan."

"All right, Mulligan, since you know. You're in a special category. It's up to you whether you let Raxby in on the secret. Normally, as far as I'm concerned, a chap's past is his own affair. No, I wasn't thinking of you. It's Wheeler, Landers—and probably Conway. They've got other problems."

"Such as?" Raxby again.

"They're what in the trade is loosely called pathological, old boy. Crazy, if you like—sometimes, in certain ways. Look, I'm not a chemist, much less a medico. But I did a spell in a mental hospital, once. And drugs could be very tricky. The damned things sometimes went into reverse. A patient would climb on the roof naked every morning before breakfast, so he'd be prescribed a tranquilizer to calm him down. Result—until they found the right medication, the right dose, he'd race around in his birthday suit trying to take a dive out of a fifth floor window. Do you follow?"

O'Malley said, "I suppose they told you everything about us?"

Bainbridge looked away. "Yes, of course. I practically went blind reading your files, and that brings me to the crunch. We're in dangerous company. Wheeler's a killer. He can't help it, of course, but that doesn't make it pretty. He was what they called my Special Study at college. They had him in an institution for a while. I used to go there twice a week, trying to interview Wheeler, befriend Wheeler. What a joke! I could have made a jollier playmate of a rattlesnake. Then there's Landers, pyromaniac, compulsive arsonist—only it isn't just that. Every now and again when there's a full moon he goes completely off his head, thinks fire is the only thing that will purify the soul. Somebody else's soul, of course. At the last count, six old people died in a burned out flat in Bristol."

A short silence. Still no sound outside.

O'Malley said, "In my case, it's simple. Drinking the water Skeel found, being able to keep off the milk for a day or two. As I was telling Raxby, that's what temporarily broke the drug's hold. It accounts for my only half remembering . . . doesn't it?"

Bainbridge nearly laughed. "Afraid not, old boy. You mean, you thought their wonder drug was in the milk? Nothing so simple, I'm afraid. It was a long course, with the final shot straight up the rectum, before you ever arrived here."

Raxby had half a cupful left on Travers' locker. He glared at it suspiciously as Bainbridge went on, "Drink up, Raxby, if you want to. There's nothing in it now, so far as I know. There never was, apart from a mixture of pep pills and knock-out drops. I was told to shove them in—to keep you all fairly quiet and happy. I didn't bother with the last churn—didn't seem a lot of point. I gave Connie a few shots, that was all. Before that, it is just possible that too many cooks spoiled the broth. Or possibly the mistake 'God' made, or the Home Office, was to try mixing delinquency with dementia. I wouldn't know."

"How do you know Wheeler remembers you?" asked Raxby.

"He called me Smithy."

"And Landers?"

"It was the way he looked at the matches."

"So what next?"

"I can get you out, I think. Through the vaults."

"Keep it, mate. I'd be no more than a zombie."

"Your choice, Raxby. And yours, O'Malley—or Mulligan."

Raxby said, "I take it *I've* got a real name?"

"Yes . . . but you can wait for it."

"How long?"

Bainbridge took the hypodermic from his pocket. "About half an hour. This, my lads, is what is known to modern science as an antidote. Unfortunately, Wheeler has one, too. I'm not sure he'll know where to stick it, but Landers will. His IQ's a hundred and fifty."

O'Malley said, "And you think they'll try giving the others a dose?"

"Yes, if it occurs to their wayward minds. I rather hope they don't reach Miller's bottom, though. Did I forget to mention it? Millie and Connie are brothers. Would you believe it? Their names are David and Jonathan! And Millie—that's David, tried to kill Connie—that's Jonathan —by putting caustic acid in his milk."

"Christ!" said Raxby. "So he's crazy too?"

"You think so?"

"That stuff—what's it called?—give us a shot quick."

"Are you sure you want it, Raxby?"

"Yes, I'm sure."

"You, O'Malley? It may put you back where you were, with all the gaps filled in."

O'Malley's eyes dropped. Then, with a sharp look at Raxby, he rolled up his left sleeve. Raxby saw the scabs, turned his eyes away.

And O'Malley said, "What's the use? So I'm scarred— and maybe I will be again. But we *are* our scars, man.

That's what makes us human. You don't get rid of them by forgetting, perhaps only by remembering. You aren't saved by having your self destroyed, obliterated—but by living with it, knowing it deeper and deeper, longer and longer, until you can say, yes, this is me . . . Mulligan, not such a great guy, but *me*. Do I really want something else—to be a zombie, as Raxby says?"

Bainbridge bestirred himself. He took the syringe from its box and carefully checked the fluid level. He thought he heard the first sounds above—from the chapel?

Apparently O'Malley heard them, too. "We shouldn't leave you—on your own."

"That's what I'm paid for."

"What?" asked Raxby. "A hundred thousand a year?"

"Less tax."

Raxby's eyes narrowed. "You're going to let us go—just like that?"

"Just like that. If you get out through the vaults, keep clear of the woods across the field. They're waiting there. I wouldn't call them a Panzer division, but they could be a nuisance. Drop your trousers and bend over, Raxby. This is going to hurt you more than it hurts me."

17

BAINBRIDGE FOUND THE CHAPEL DOOR BARRED AGAINST him. He put his shoulder to it and at last it gave, inch by inch, held back from its full swing by some obstruction behind.

He squeezed through, kicking away the shifted pews and rubbish and looked toward the altar.

Someone—Landers?—had lit candles on it, several along the rail. Beyond the flickering flames was a slit of light and the movement of a shadow. The sacristy! Either he'd forgotten to close the door behind him or they'd managed to break in. Why, though? What was there for them, now?

The communicating door, of course! Even if the lock did defeat Landers, a few good thumps might bring Father Ignatius and his band of Brothers running—to get a jet of tear gas in their faces and open the way to an unscheduled escape?

Bainbridge knew they'd seen him, heard him break in. Nobody called, but suddenly the wheelchair, empty, came straight at him. Half thrown, half pushed, it careened across the sanctuary, smashing through the rail and spilling lighted candles.

One still flickered on the altar steps. Bainbridge stamped it out, then dropped to his knees and made for cover behind a choir stall.

He had a better view from there: sacristy door wide open, Wheeler looking for him in the gloom, tear gas tube held like a tommy gun. No Hackett, no Landers . . . but Miller and Conway. Conway was squatting in a corner, Miller kneeling beside him. When and how had they got those two up here? He should have checked Miller's cell, got them out in time . . . and where was Landers?

A blinding jet of tear gas struck the choir stalls, hanging like a poison cloud. Bainbridge choked, clawed at his eyes. And as he tried to crawl out of range, he suddenly knew where Landers was. By the chapel door, by the pile of wood and cardboard!

Then the flames . . . flames rising with an awful efflorescence. They mushroomed against the doors, swallowing their own smoke. The base of the fire became a crackling red amoeba, dividing itself, sending out little tongues of new life to nourish themselves on anything they could take hold of.

Bainbridge stamped among them, choking, shoes already smoldering, hands and face scorching. He drifted blindly toward the crumbling, molten cliff as it sent brilliant tendrils clutching at the roof beams . . .

Landers stood very close to his latest creation. His body felt nothing; the new-born fires at his feet were footlights and like a good actor, he paid no attention to the hazy faces beyond.

Was this, perhaps, what he had always wanted? A final act, a consummation?

He stared with fascination at what he had brought to pass: Landers with his power to paint the sky red, splash walls with crimson, sketch ghastly faces staring like apoplexies from high windows.

Landers' terrible dragon had broken from its leash at last, and it brought not horror, but a delight as twisted as melting girders.

So Landers did not recoil. He would await the sound of the juggernaut, watch the blue fire-fly light twinkle round the corner—but first he would address those unseen faces: "But don't you see? Don't you *understand* . . . ?"

Hackett's thoughts were more simple, if less profound. "Get out of this, mate. Out—fast!"

He remembered nobody, thought of nobody, only Hackett. And no fire some crazy fool had started would reach him in time.

Hackett, the cheerful burglar, now remembered his proud reputation: the youngest professional catman in the business!

He knotted his shoes about his neck and climbed like a spider. The loose tiles were no tighter than he'd once left them and, now that he knew who he was and where he was heading, he had no trouble pushing them aside.

An innocuous curl of smoke followed him out on to the roof. Yeah, it was much as he'd guessed. No drainpipe. Who needed drainpipes? Pushed to it, Hackett would make a fifty foot drop into a barrel of sawdust!

Skeel reached the top of his climb. Skeel was still just Skeel and he had his cat with him.

He knew where the cat belonged and to whom it belonged. The cat, however, seemed to have forgotten again. So, with the way things were going, the things he'd picked up from the other blokes lately, Skeel had decided to drop him back home. You could drop cats quite a long way, couldn't you? You didn't break their legs or nothing.

At the top of the belfry tower, Skeel stayed on all fours, doing nothing for some time, eyes turned up at the bright hollow of the big bell. The sun made him squint.

The bell was a bit like a flower, he thought. A giant, silvery-brown flower with a hammer dangling down in the middle—that was like in a flower, too.

When his eyes were used to the light, he stood up slowly and leaned on the edge, squeezing his cat. He saw the fields ripening in the sun, trees sharp against the sky. He heard the bleating of sheep and the disgruntled low of cows with full udders.

A man with a stick and a dog was bringing them to the shed, the one near the cottage. Skeel watched them all go into the shed. By the noise they made inside you'd think it was a slaughter house!

The girl came out of the cottage, as he guessed she would because she'd have seen him from the window. Pretty, friendly, never asked a lot of daft questions—at least after Skeel had made it clear she wasn't getting any answers!

But today she looked anxious, hair dancing in the breeze as she hurried toward the wall of the monastery.

She came to the foot of the tower, all of thirty feet down. Without any 'hello' or anything, she said, "This time you've *got* to jump."

"Can't," said Skeel. "Ain't got wings."

"Look!" said the girl.

There was a thick, soft mat of straw at the foot of the tower. Skeel hadn't got round to noticing it.

"You're on fire, did you know?"

"Who, me??"

"No, you silly—that place. We saw smoke ages ago. Dad phoned the fire brigade. They'll be there in a minute. You can't go back. Jump!"

"Can't," said Skeel. "Look, I've got your cat. I told you I'd bring him. *He* can jump."

"Throw him down first, then come after."

The cat wasn't at all keen. It wriggled and tried to scratch. Skeel held it over the belfry edge and dropped it. It miaowed frantically all the way down, then landed on the straw heap and scuttled off with its ears back.

"Now you," said the girl.

Skeel hesitated. He could smell the smoke, now—it was pouring out of his belfry! But he shook his head. "You don't want me down there. You don't know what I done." Neither did Skeel, but it had never made him feel any better—or much worse.

"Who cares? I'm going to count three, then you jump. Okay?"

She counted three. Skeel climbed up—and jumped . . .

Bainbridge was out. Scorched shoes, burnt denims. Bare arms and hands badly blistered so that on the road he held them out from his body. Hell, they stung! There was a charred hole in one leg of his denims. His face was sore, but only his beard was actually singed. He couldn't get rid of the stench of burned hair.

He should have gone in the ambulance for a checkup. But here he was, a burnt scarecrow sick of minding the farmer's potato patch.

Before him lay a long stretch of open road, not much traffic. Evening was coming on, the sun as red as fire. On his right, beyond a cornfield, hung a pall of smoke. Bainbridge scarcely gave it a glance.

Then, although he'd not been looking, he saw them sitting on a bank by the side of the road. Two of them. "Why are you still hanging about here? The area's thick with police patrols."

They glared up at him. O'Malley, eyes faintly puzzled, cheek twitching. Raxby's face totally blank.

Raxby seemed to be trying to work something out. "Hitching a lift. They never gave us no money. What went wrong—the blaze? You usually get a five-pound note at least. Stingy bleeders!"

O'Malley glanced down at Bainbridge's arms. "You're in a bad way, chum."

"It's nothing."

A long, probing stare back—but it was not enough.

Raxby had lost interest. He was looking up the road in the direction of the oncoming traffic. It was a toss-up which arrived first, an accommodating truck or a patrol car.

Luck was with them, though—for the moment. A large truck was approaching, and Raxby was in the middle of the road flagging it down. The truck slowed, easing onto the berm. The driver's mate leaned out and said, "Climb in the back and don't try lifting any of the freight."

Bainbridge said, "But hang on . . ."

Raxby misunderstood. "Don't crowd us, mate. Beat it and find your own lift."

And they were gone. O'Malley waved vaguely from the back of the truck.

Bainbridge sat on the grassy bank, burnt arms outstretched. He laughed—laughed aloud.

What a foul-up! Somebody at the Home Office was sure to be fired. And Father Ignatius hadn't needed Wheeler's squirt of gas to bring tears to his eyes. Them and their wonder drug!

Its antidote was even more wonderful! It had left them in a different valley of forgetfulness—the fugue state! Everything that had happened during the "treatment" wiped out!

So they were all back to square one. Raxby, even O'Malley, hadn't recognized him. They hadn't even known each other, just met by accident on the road, teaming up on the strength of that drifting smoke across the cornfield. Poor old Raxby even thought he'd been officially released from somewhere!

Wheeler had come out, dragging David and Jonathan with him—through the door in the sacristy. But what about Skeel and Hackett? Only Landers had been found so far. How many spines had he managed to inject first!

And how many days would they live their old agony before they were all locked up again? In the meantime would Raxby blow his top and smash in yet another face, O'Malley pitch what was left of his self-respect against a different hypodermic, Miller with his damaged sibling's mind go after Connie in his sleep . . . ?

Perhaps the Home Office had an antidote for their antidote! Bainbridge felt guilty, of course. But they had given him something impossible to do, and you always felt guilty if you failed. They had wanted him to walk on water and—in the end, he'd grabbed a boat. It didn't excuse him that the voyage hadn't been for himself.

Bainbridge, alias Smith, looked at his arms, and they stung like hell. Christ, how they stung—like arms spread on a tree.

Funny . . . you had to laugh!

Bainbridge cried. He cried solid for ten minutes, tears smarting on his burned arms.

Then, at last, an observant truck driver pulled over to

the side of the road. "Trouble, mate? Want a lift some-where? Can take you as far as Knightsbridge."

He'd be wanted at Landers' inquest. He'd be wanted by the Order, to give an account of himself, to explain. They were *all* wanted now.

Bainbridge looked up and said, "Thanks."

He climbed into the cab.